I0564574

UNDER A BLOODRED SKY

Avigdor Hameiri's
War Stories
and Poetry

UNDER A BLOODRED SKY

Avigdor Hameiri's War Stories and Poetry

Edited and Translated
by Peter C. Appelbaum
and Dan Hecht

BOSTON
2023

Library of Congress Cataloging-in-Publication Data

Names: Hameiri, Avigdor, 1890-1970, author. | Appelbaum, Peter C., editor,
  translator. | Hecht, Dan, 1982—editor, translator.
Title: Under a bloodred sky : Avigdor Hameiri's war stories and poetry /
  Avigdor Hameiri ; edited and translated by Peter C. Appelbaum and Dan Hecht.
Other titles: Under a bloodred sky (Compilation)
Description: Boston : Academic Studies Press, 2023. | Includes
  bibliographical references.
Identifiers: LCCN 2022055773 (print) | LCCN 2022055774 (ebook) |
  ISBN 9798887190662 (hardback) | ISBN 9798887190679 (paperback) |
  ISBN 9798887190686 (adobe pdf) | ISBN 9798887190693 (epub)
Subjects: LCSH: Hameiri, Avigdor, 1890-1970—Translations into English. |
  LCGFT: War fiction. | War poetry. | Short stories. | Poetry.
Classification: LCC PJ5053.H3 U53 2023 (print) | LCC PJ5053.H3 (ebook) |
  DDC 892.43/5—dc23/eng/20221129
LC record available at https://lccn.loc.gov/2022055773
LC ebook record available at https://lccn.loc.gov/2022055774

Copyright, English translation and introductions © 2023 Academic Studies Press.
All rights reserved.

ISBN 9798887190662 (hardback)
ISBN 9798887190679 (paperback)
ISBN 9798887190686 (Adobe PDF)
ISBN 9798887190693 (ePub)

Book design by Tatiana Vernikov
Cover design by Ivan Grave
On the cover: Yohanan Petrovsky-Shtern, "Fall of the Empire,"
  acrylic on canvas, 36×36 inches, 2018. Reproduced by permission.

Published by Cherry Orchard Books, and imprint of Academic Studies Press
1577 Beacon St.
Brookline, MA 02446, USA
press@academicstudiespress.com
www.academicstudiespress.com

Contents

Introduction
by Editors and Translators

This anthology of short stories and poetry follows the publication of four other texts by Avigdor Hameiri in translations by Peter Appelbaum.[1] Hameiri wrote in almost every conceivable form, and much of his work has either never been published or published only once in periodical form. His war stories are unique, and different from his Hebrew writer contemporaries in that they mix the supernatural and macabre with war, pogroms, and antisemitism. Hameiri was one of the only contemporary Hebrew writers to incorporate these styles in his writings, which did not gain him many friends. We have compiled an anthology of ten each of Hameiri's most compelling war stories and poems—some of which were only published once in periodical form in the early 1920s.[2] These stories and poems reflect like no other the unique complexity of the Jewish soldier's experience of the most vicious and shocking war the world had yet witnessed—the battles, the agony, the dilemmas faced by the Jewish soldier, bravery versus cowardice, the notion of imminent death, breaking the sixth commandment (Thou Shalt Not Murder), elements of pacifism (particularly involving camaraderie between the common soldiers on both sides of the battlefield and their shared hatred for rank), and more. As mentioned, Hameiri delved deep into the inferno, was not afraid of graphic depictions of war, and did so in groundbreaking supernatural and fantastic literature. Up to that point in Jewish and Hebrew literature, this kind of writing was confined to myths like the those of the dybbuk or the golem, but the killing fields of

---

1   Avigdor Hameiri, *Hell on Earth*, trans. Peter C. Appelbaum (Detroit, MI: Wayne State University Press, 2017); idem, *Of Human Carnage—Odessa 1918-1920*, trans. Peter C. Appelbaum (Middletown, RI: Stone Tower Press and Boston, MA: Black Widow Press, 2020); idem, *Voyage into Savage Europe: A Declining Civilization*, trans. Peter C. Appelbaum (Boston, MA: Academic Studies Press, 2020); idem, *The Great Madness*, trans. and ed. Peter C. Appelbaum (Middletown, RI: Stone Tower Press and Boston, MA: Black Widow Press, 2021).

2   Some of stories and poems in this anthology were republished in Avigdor Hameiri, *Sipurei Milhama* (Tel Aviv: Am Oved, 1970).

the Eastern Front provided Hameiri an abundance of chilling horror stories, which unsettled many readers who read them in the original Hebrew approximately one hundred years ago.

"Christians" is a story of barbarism, summarized in *The Great Madness*.[3] At first glance, it may seem fantastic, but perusal of reports of the Khmelnytsky massacres and subsequent Cossack pogroms reveal acts of savagery as bad, if not worse, against the entire civilian Jewish population, including women and children. In 1913 in Kiev, Menachem Mendel Beilis was accused of ritual murder and blood libel, so this antisemitic legal theater would, presumably, have been fresh in people's minds when the story was published in early 1916. Hameiri's out-of-body experience, first mentioned in "Christians," is repeated in "On the Verge" (see below). The over-the-top cruelty is in reality a plea for pacifism.

"Revenge" is a dark tale of human conflict. The story probes the depths of Hameiri's soul, which is torn between the land of his birth and his spiritual homeland (see also the poem "My Two Souls").[4] But there is an added conflict: Hungarian virtuoso violonist Freidi's right hand is Christian and his left hand is instinctively Jewish. Amputate his left hand, and you remove the gift of music that is the hallmark of the Jewish soul—after all, most of the great violinists of the 150 years prior to the story's setting were Jewish. Freidi is eventually strangled by his amputated left hand, that is, his own Jewish soul. The assimilated Jews of Hungary, try as they might, couldn't escape their Jewish origins. This story, published in 1921, resembles Maurice Renard's novel *Les Mains d'Orlac* (*The Hands of Orlac*) (1920),[5] on which the movie *The Hands of Orlac* (1924) was based.

"On the Verge" is a bizarre story about a prophetic dream Hameiri had. The names of dead and murdered men and a woman combine with an-out-of-body experience on the battlefield during which he is an immortal soul, immune from the enemy's weapons. Like "Christians," it emphasizes Cossack brutality, as opposed to supranational peace, tranquility, and pacifism.

"The Spider" is loosely based on the story of the same name by the German writer of the macabre Hanns Heinz Ewers whom Hameiri knew very

---

3   Hameiri, *The Great Madness*, 228-238.

4   Hameiri, *Voyage into Savage Europe*, 114.

5   Maurice Renard, *Les Mains d'Orlac* (Paris: Nilsson, 1920).

well,[6] but with a Jewish twist. The spider is a metaphor for the commandant who ensnares the protagonist Walter Amudi in his web of antisemitic hate. This, despite (or because of) Amudi's proven bravery in the face of danger.

"A Blessed Fall Dawn," the only story in the anthology of an unabashedly gentle nature, describes the lengths taken by Uncle Osterreicher, an Orthodox Jew more fully described in *The Great Madness*, to be able to recite kaddish on the anniversary of his wife's death. He is completely aware that there are many Jews on the Russian side in the war, and enlists their help to obtain a prayer *minyan*.[7] This story reflects the dilemma in which Jews on opposing sides found themselves during World War I. Nearly one million Jews served in the armies of all the belligerents, and often found themselves fighting each other. Orthodox Jews fought just as fiercely as their assimilated brethren, sometimes going into battle clad in tallit and tefillin.

"Hanale" is a macabre story of death and transfiguration. The protagonist, engaged to a young yeshiva student, escapes a lascivious Cossack whose people have killed her parents only to fall back into his clutches in the blazing inferno of a Jewish cemetery. Her dead fiancé is found grasping her amputated arm with the engagement ring on its finger.

"Night of Vigil" depicts six shrouded men celebrating a Pesach seder at the front, immune from enemy fire, intoning the prayer to welcome the prophet Elijah, which is in effect a curse on non-Jews' injustice towards Jews. The visiting major may represent the Angel of Death wanting his own (Jewish) soldiers to die; but God strikes him down. This story parallels a chapter from the best-selling novel *The Moon of Israel* (1918) by H. Rider Haggard (1856-1925), which retells the story of the Exodus from the viewpoint of an Egyptian prince and his Jewish slave girl sweetheart. A high-ranking Egyptian soldier breaks into the first Pesach seder, mocks the prince and the Jews, drinks a sacred cup of wine, and then drops dead outside the slave quarters. The story was adapted into a screenplay in 1922 by the Hungarian screenwriter Ladislaus Vajda (1877-1933) and later produced in Vienna as the epic movie

---

6   Hanns Heinz Ewers (1871-1943), German actor, poet, philosopher, and writer of short stories and novels; now known mainly for his works of horror, particularly his trilogy of novels about the adventures of Frank Braun, a character modeled on himself. The best known of these is *Alraune* (1911). See Hanns Heinz Ewers, *Strange Tales*, Wilfried Kugel, copyright (Bastrop, TX: Lodestar, 2014), 103-120.

7   Quorum of ten adult men necessary for communal prayer.

Die Sklavenkönigin (Moon of Israel) in 1924, directed by another Hungarian, Mihaly Kertész (later Michael Curtiz [1886-1962]).

"Storm" is an interesting literary take on the process of phagocytosis, which was discovered by Ilya Mechnikov. In the story, blood circulation is described as a circle, leukocytes as spheres with eyes, and bacteria as snakes spitting poison. In *The Great Madness*, Hameiri recounts how he read a book by Mechnikov on his way to the front in August 1914, so he must have been well aware of the zoologist's work.[8] Mechnikov and Paul Ehrlich shared the Nobel Prize for Medicine in 1908 for their pioneering work in the field of the nascent science of immunology.[9] Hameiri perhaps entitles this story "Storm" because of Theodor Körner's famous statement during the Napoleonic Wars: "Now people rise up, and storm break loose."[10]

"Sarah Bänger" is a story about the depths of depravity into which a previously normal person may be driven by a bad upbringing and cruelty during childhood and young adulthood. Sarah Bänger's experiments with corpses recall those conducted in Auschwitz and other concentration camps. There is also a Frankenstein-like element. In the novel by Mary Shelley (1797-1851) published in 1818, Dr. Frankenstein experiments on dead bodies. Furthermore, the area in which Hameiri was born and brought up was well acquainted with vampire legends, as well as those of the "blood-drinking" Elizabeth Báthory.[11] There is also a hint of potential necrophilia. It isn't clear whether the mutilated corpse at the end of the story is really that of Bänger's father.

"Gift," a novelette in four parts about antisemitism, brutality, the spirit world, and the survival of the just, was torn up by Shaul Tschernichowsky when he read it.[12] Its macabre nature obviously grated on the sensibilities of this poet who loved Greek art and aesthetics. Hameiri's posthumous papers

---

8   Hameiri, *The Great Madness*, 88.

9   Ilya Ilyich Mechnikov (1845-1916) and Paul Ehrlich (1854-1915), Russian and German pioneers in the field of immunology.

10   Theodor Körner (1791-1813), German poet who died fighting in the Napoleonic Wars; famous for his statement *"Nun Volk steh auf und Sturm brich los,"* which was notoriously used by Goebbels in his 1944 Sportpalast speech.

11   Elizabeth Báthory (1560-1614), Hungarian noblewoman reputed to have bathed in the blood of virgins. No reliable proof for this has been found.

12   Shaul Tschernichowsky (1875-1943), Russian-born Hebrew poet, considered one of the great Modern Hebrew poets; he is considered a nature poet and was greatly influenced by the culture of ancient Greece.

show that the editor of *Hashiloah*, Joseph Klausner, was reluctant to publish it. The novelette foretells the use made by the Nazis of the more "traditional" crimes against Jews, that is, humiliation, antisemitic Christian myths, and the "staging" of the killing of Jews. The roasted baby on a plate comes straight out of Ewers, but there is a great deal more to the story than that. It is suffused with the Faust legend, and Heine's "Der Doppelgänger." Hameiri knew Heine's work well—indeed he translated some of his poetry into Hebrew.[13]

In the story, Piotr Ilyich and Fräulein de Barbanel, who are Baroness Medusa von Schinken's alter egos, come to warn her of her impending doom. The end of the story bears an uncanny resemblance to Wilde's *The Picture of Dorian Gray* (1891), another variant on the Faust legend.[14] The train hurtling to the cemetery reminds the reader of the rider in Goethe's "Der Erlkönig,"[15] and the chilling cloud on a moonlight night is reminiscent of Poe's "Annabel Lee."[16] Hameiri was well aware of these authors and their works. Dr. Domshivski the local physician epitomizes the savagery of Cossack antisemitism and Jewish murder. In Jewish historical memory, Bohdan Khmelnytsky is second only to Adolf Hitler as a murderer of Jews. Ivan Gonta, mentioned in the story, was another Cossack murderer of Jews and Poles.[17] This story was written in Odessa, where Hameiri was a first-hand witness of the anti-Jewish pogroms that took place during the Russian Civil War. Depending on the source to which

---

13 Heinrich Heine (1797-1856), German poet, writer, and literary critic. He is best known outside Germany for his early lyric poetry. See Heinrich Heine, *Ne'imot Ivriot*, trans. Avigdor Hameiri (Tel Aviv: Sinai, 1948).

14 Oscar Wilde (1854-1900), Irish poet and playwright.

15 Johann Wolfgang von Goethe (1749-1832), one of Germany's greatest authors and poets; also a statesman, scientist, and philosopher. Author of *Faust*.

16 Edgar Allan Poe (1809-1849), American writer, poet, editor, and literary critic.

17 Zynoviy Bohdan Khmelnytsky (c. 1595-1657), Hetman of the Zaporozhian Host, then in the Polish Crown of the Polish Lithuanian-Commonwealth (now part of Ukraine). He led an uprising against the commonwealth and its magnates (1648–1654) that resulted in the creation of a state led by the Cossacks. During this war, between eighteen thousand and one hundred thousand Jews were killed, some with appalling savagery. As managers of their estates and collectors of their taxes, Jews were the face of the hated Polish aristocracy. Ivan Gonta (d. 1768), a successor to Khmelnytsky, led a rebellion against the voivode of Kiev; he and his militia joined the rebels, and the joint forces captured and ravaged the town of Uman on June 21, 1768. In what became known as the Massacre of Uman, thousands of local Polish nobles, Jews, Uniates, and others were slaughtered.

one refers, thirty-five thousand to more than one hundred thousand Jews were killed.

Hameiri's speech to a 1935 Antifa (Antifascist) party conference summarizes how his political beliefs changed with time. He ended the war a convinced pacifist. When he arrived in Israel, he was at first attracted to Revisionism,[18] but the group moved too far to the right and he became a Socialist with Marxist tendencies. He tells the audience that most of them have no concept of war and its terrors or the terrible cruelty of officers who despise their men and abuse them at every turn. The faction in Mandatory Palestine that sees advantages in fascism such as that practiced by Mussolini recommends war, but Hameiri is emphatically against it. There is no beauty in war, only misery, suffering and hatred. The audience should not allow themselves to be misled by slogans. The plutocrats want to brainwash people and use them as cannon fodder in wars that make arms manufacturers vast profits. Hameiri concludes: "We must scream with all our strength, and whisper burning words in each other's ears, against a war for such 'culture' and 'ideals.' Don't go! Don't go! Don't go! Better to die on the spot than go there to die or to return like a leprous dog, waiting for the next war, living and dying like a leprous dog!"

Avigdor Hameiri (in 1914, still Feuerstein) had joined the war effort already an accomplished Hebrew poet. His book *Mi-shire Avigdor Foyershtayn: Kovets Rishon* received much attention due to its modernist qualities, a result of his friendships with key Hungarian poets such as Endre Adi (1877-1919) and Frigyes Karinthy (1887-1938).[19] The horrors of war and captivity left an indelible mark on his life and writing. Hameiri's poetry is gruesome and unforgiving. He saw the suffering, mutilation, death, and dying around him—the slaughter of an entire generation of Europe's best and brightest young men—and nobody in authority seemed to care. This anthology includes ten

---

18 Revisionist Zionism was an ideology developed by Ze'ev Jabotinsky who advocated a "revision" of the "practical Zionism" of David Ben Gurion and Chaim Weizmann which was focused on the settling of *Eretz Yisrael* (Land of Israel) by independent individuals. Revisionism differed from other types of Zionism primarily in its territorial maximalism. Revisionists insisted upon the Jewish right to sovereignty over the whole of *Eretz Yisrael*, which they equated to Mandatory Palestine and Transjordan. It was the chief ideological competitor to the dominant socialist Labor Zionism. In his speech to "Antifa," Hameiri mistakenly calls Jabotinsky the leader of fascism in Mandatory Palestine.

19 Avigdor Hameiri, *Mi-shire Avigdor Foyershtayn: Kovets Rishon* (Budapest: Histadrut HaZionim beHungaria, 1911).

remarkable poems of war and captivity, translated into English for the first time: some have been lost in crumbling, yellow-paged periodicals, destined for oblivion. In many of the poems, nature looks on at the indiscriminate destruction from under a bloodred sky. Soldiers see their comrades writhing and roasting in a pit of suffering—but they don't care, Instead, they light a cigar and go out to lunch, delivering their fate to a laughing God. While men suffer, plutocrats and war profiteers get rich from human suffering. The sun shines in the heavens, satiated ravens and vultures fly around the rotting corpses, but civilians, war profiteers and other privileged people lie sleeping in their comfortable beds unconcerned and oblivious. In the dugouts, all manner of insects fly around, gorging themselves on the dead and spreading disease. Rats are everywhere, feasting on the dead and even gnawing on the living. Soldiers with pneumonia and tuberculosis cough up blood. Water leaks in from outside, and men huddle together, brothers in shared misery. Hameiri lies asleep, king of the filth. Do not look into the eyes of a dying man as you kill him, lest your blood and bones become forever poisoned and your body freezes. The sun shines on flowers and insects mating in a cemetery that reeks with the stench of decomposing corpses. The Angel of Death is bade welcome by the guards on night watch and an orphan marries a groom of death. Hameiri berates mother for sending their children to war. Ernst Toller, another pacifist poet (in the German language) who served in the war, similarly addresses German mothers, hoping that their pain may give rise to shared humanity after the war.[20] The gruesome description of soldiers with disfigured faces mirrors *Emah Gedolah ve'Yareach* (Great Fear and the Moon) by Uri Zvi Greenberg.[21]

These are not easy stories and poems to read, and they not for the faint of heart; but we are convinced of their value. We thank the Shapira brothers for copyright approval to publish another volume of their grandfather's works; Yohanan Petrovsky Shtern for permission to use one of his own paintings for the book cover; Tamar Drukker for gracing the anthology with a scholarly introduction; Dana Robbins for her helpful feedback on the poetry; and Addie Appelbaum for valued assistance with film and other references. Finally, we

20   Peter C. Appelbaum and James W. Scott, eds., *Broken Carousel. German Jewish Soldier-Poets of the Great War* (Newport RI: Stone Tower Books, 2017), 350-351.

21   See Peter C. Appelbaum, *Habsburg Sons: Jews in the Austro-Hungarian Army 1788-1918* (Boston, MA: Academic Studies Press, 2022), 146.

would like to thank Alessandra Anzani, Stuart Allen, and Kira Nemirovsky of Academic Studies Press for their usual insightful advice and assistance. Any errors in the text are ours alone.

—*Peter C. Appelbaum, Land o' Lakes, FL*
—*Dan Hecht, Tel Aviv, Israel*

November 2021

Introduction

In the summer of 1914, when the soldiers of the Austro-Hungarian army marched into battle in the Balkans, they did so singing the patriotic "Austrian Cavalry Song":

> There in the meadow-land
> Two jackdaws cry—
> Is it on Danube's strand
> I'll have to die?
> Or in a Polish grave?
> Before my soul shall fly,
> I'll fight a rider brave.
>
> . . . .
>
> There in the evening breath
> Hover two crows:
> When comes the reaper Death
> Who mows and mows?
> We're not afraid!
> If but our banner blows
> Over Belgrade![1]

The verse, put to music by Franz Lehár, was written by Hugo Zuckermann in 1914 and captured the strong nationalist patriotism and enthusiasm for war, typical for the early months of the conflict.

Hugo Zuckermann was born in 1881 in Cheb (Czech Republic), to an assimilated Jewish family. Antisemitism, on the one hand, and the rise of Zionism, on the other, brought him to embrace and learn more about his heritage. He translated Jewish short stories and plays from Yiddish to German, and established a Jewish theater in Vienna. He was also a strong supporter of

---

1   Hugo Zuckermann, "Österreichisches Reiterlied," in *A Harvest of German Verse*, ed. and trans. Margarete Münsterberg (New York and London: D. Appleton and Company, 1917), 233.

Zionism. However, as "Austrian Cavalry Song" attests, he also identified as an Austrian nationalist—a patriot. Like many of his contemporaries and coreligionists, he enlisted in 1914 and was killed in battle in December 1914. Zuckermann was thirty-three years old at the outbreak of the war.

A lawyer by profession and a poet and dramatist, he did not consider military service as a vocation, until the outbreak of the war. However, mass conscription in 1914 and in the following years to support the war effort resulted in an army that comprised almost every male member of society—men from most age groups, all backgrounds, and of every ability. In this respect, it was the very first total war. Zuckermann and his contemporaries willingly joined the army to participate in what soon became a continent-wide conflagration, but their nationalist fervor was not racial: it was cultural. The poem illustrates the cultural impact of national rhetoric on the citizens of Europe, whom the war was to impact dramatically.

The Great War was the largest and most devastating conflict in history until then, costing the lives of more than eight million soldiers on all sides, and almost a similar number of civilian casualties across Europe, and beyond. The war changed Europe. It changed the map, it changed demography, it changed social structures, it changed language. All these changes were reflected in the culture formed by and that emerged from this bloodbath. The Great War was also unprecedented in its literary impact, with the thousands of established and future writers who took part in, and were directly affected by, the war writing about their experiences.

In the late eighteenth century, Jewish emancipation under the Habsburg monarchy led to introduction of military service for Jews across the Austro-Hungarian Empire. Jews enlisted and fought alongside their Christians fellow nationals for over a century before the outbreak of the Great War. However, 1914 saw a real change in scale. Approximately a million Jews took part in this war, on both sides of the conflict. Of these, over three hundred thousand Jewish soldiers served in the Austro-Hungarian army, some twenty-five thousand of them as reserve officers.[2] The conflict also impacted greatly on the lives of Jews living in areas between the warring sides and constantly overrun by opposing armies.

---

2   Peter C. Appelbaum, *Habsburg Sons: Jews in the Austro-Hungarian Army, 1788-1918* (Boston, MA: Academic Studies Press, 2022).

Like Hugo Zuckermann, there were other recruits who chose the pen to document and creatively respond to the horrors they underwent and witnessed. Particularly interesting are Jewish writers whose creative response to the war was in Hebrew, rather than one of the European tongues in which the war was fought and experienced. Choosing to write in a language that was not one of the vernaculars of the war experience turns even the most factual account into a creative literary work. Glenda Abramson's *Hebrew Writing of the First World War*[3] offers a comprehensive and detailed study of the literature of the Great War in Hebrew, from works composed by soldiers in the European battlefield and Jewish civilians in Europe, to those experiencing the war between the British and the Ottoman powers in Palestine. Of these Jewish Hebrew writers, Avigdor Hameiri (Feuerstein) stands out for his extensive war literature and for its importance in his overall oeuvre.[4]

With a literary career spanning from 1907, with the publication of his first Hebrew poem, to his death in Tel Aviv in 1970, Hameiri is best remembered for his expressionist poetry and his theater work, mostly satire. A significant share of his literary production is his war literature, which includes two docu-novels, a play, almost thirty short stories, and about fifty poems, as well as translations and adaptations of war literature by other European writers, from Hašek's *The Good soldier Švejk* (a dramatization was staged in Hebrew in 1935) to Ben-Gavriel's *Gold in the Streets* (1946).

Avigdor Hameiri was born Avigdor Feuerstein in 1890 in Újdávidháza in the Trans-Carpathian region, then a part of Hungary, and was brought up in his grandfather's house, where he received a traditional Jewish education and learned to read and write in Hebrew. As a young man, he moved to study in a yeshiva in Budapest. It was in the city, outside the religious house of study, where he was exposed to the ideas of Jewish nationalism and became active in Zionist circles. At the same time, he also began to establish himself as a writer in Hungarian and formed strong links to other contemporary poets and writers. He befriended the Jewish Zionist writer and activist József Patai (1882-1953), as well as the renowned Hungarian poet Endre Ady (1877-1919), and both these writers had a lasting influence on Hameiri and his writing. Throughout his life, Hameiri found himself identified and identifying with

---

3   Glenda Abramson, *Hebrew Writing of the First World War* (London and Portland, OR: Vallentine Mitchell, 2008).

4   Ibid., 3-67.

Jewish and Zionist ideology, as well as Hungarian nationalism. These did not seem to be in contradiction to a form of Central European cosmopolitanism and self-awareness as a citizen of the world. This complex identity is clearly reflected in his war literature, as a constant tension between contradictory selves. National loyalty, Zionist aspirations, and European pacifist ideology: all three are present in his life, his identity, and his writings.[5]

At the outbreak of the war, Hameiri was already a published Hebrew poet and worked as a journalist for a Hungarian paper based in Budapest. He volunteered for military service, and after a brief spell on the Eastern Front was trained as an officer and returned to the trenches on the Eastern Front where he served until he was taken prisoner by the Russian forces in the autumn of 1916. He survived prisoner of war camps in Russia and Siberia, and was released after the Russian Revolution.[6] He eventually was transferred to Kiev, and arrived in Odessa, where there was already an established center for Hebrew culture and writing. He emigrated to Mandatory Palestine in 1921 and settled in Tel Aviv, where he continued to write, edit, and publish. The stories and the poems in this collection were all first published in the early 1920s, soon after his move to Tel Aviv. Gradually, he made a name for himself among the Hebrew literary circles in Mandatory Palestine. He established a Hebrew-language theater and a periodical, both serving as a platform for disseminating his own original work, as well as translations and works by others.

Like Hameiri, many of the writers responsible for the emergence of Modern Hebrew literature, and for the creation of a literary culture in a newly revived vernacular, have their roots in Europe. Through the nineteenth and into the twentieth century, there was a growing number of Hebrew poets and authors, periodicals, and publishing houses, mostly in Central and Eastern Europe. Over the first decades of the twentieth century, the creators and promotors of this literature emigrated, some to the United States, others to Palestine, and the literature, publishing houses, and readers moved with them.

---

5   Tamar S. Drukker, "Documentation and Fiction in Hameiri's Accounts of the Great War," *CLCWeb: Comparative Literature and Culture* 17, no. 3 (2015), http://docs.lib.purdue.edu/clcweb/vol17/iss3/16.

6   Hameiri's experience of the war and of captivity is described in detail in his two docu-novels *The Great Madness* and *Hell on Earth*, both available in English in recent edited translations by Peter C. Appelbaum: *Hell on Earth* (Detroit, MI: Wayne State University Press, 2017) and *The Great Madness* (Middletown, RI: Stone Tower Press and Boston, MA: Black Widow Press, 2021).

Much of the literature published in Hebrew in the 1920s and 1930s in Palestine was written by European immigrants like Hameiri, whose literary mission was to expand and experiment with writing in Modern Hebrew to reflect reality in all its complexity, as well as to document the development of a new Zionist Hebrew culture and society. As Gershon Shaked has demonstrated in his overview of the Hebrew literature of the period, "quoting from reality was a major goal of the literature in all its aspects . . . literature, which seems at first glance to exaggerate the virtues of reality, emerges as an accurate and inspirational reflection of reality."[7] Shaked goes on to cite Hameiri's novel *Tnuva* (Produce, 1934) as an example of this exaggerated realism and documentary drive. These can also be found in Hameiri's war novels. However, as mentioned previously, the choice to write in Hebrew about events that took place outside the Hebrew-speaking world turns the reportage into literary creation—what Paul Fussell terms "memoir fiction"—or docu-novels, as such texts are more commonly called.[8]

However, the collection of stories here, published in Tel Aviv in the early 1920s, belong firmly in the Europe that Hameiri has left behind. These stories are unique and interesting not only for their subject matter, but particularly for their tone and atmosphere. Rather than capture the Jewish European experience of World War I and Jewish life in its shadow, and shape it into Modern Hebrew language within the literary conventions and aesthetics of the period, Hameiri's short stories read almost like translations into Hebrew. It is not surprising, therefore, to find in 1954 a collection of these stories reprinted by Idith publishing house, which specialized in translations of European classics. Hameiri's short stories sit comfortably alongside story collections by Thomas Mann, Guy de Maupassant, Maxim Gorky, and others.[9]

It is not merely the subject matter which makes Hameiri's short stories particularly "European" and unusual among the Hebrew literature of his time; the manner of telling, the mixture of horror, the unnatural, and bleak mystery, as well as the depth of despair familiar from European gothic literature also make them stand out. The terror of the battlefield seems to play out the

---

7   Gershon Shaked, *Modern Hebrew Fiction*, trans. Yael Lotan (New Milford, CT: The Toby Press, 2000), 104.

8   Paul Fussell, *The Great War and Modern Memory* (New York: Oxford University Press, 1975), 220.

9   See, for example, the advertisement in *Al Hamishmar*, June 6, 1954, 5.

extreme possibility of pain, gruesomeness, and madness, which can only be described in terms of the literary horror story. This is particularly foreign to the poetics of Hebrew literature in Palestine in the first half of the twentieth century.

In 1942, a contemporary of Hameiri, Haim Hazaz (1889, Ukraine–1973, Jerusalem) published his short story "The Sermon." Written almost as a monologue, the speaker, Yudka, a new immigrant living and working in a Zionist farming community, possibly a kibbutz, addresses a committee or formal group, most probably members of the *Hagana*.[10] He appeals to the committee members to recognize that there is no link between Jewish history and Zionism. The Zionist ethos of national regeneration in the land of Israel requires a break away from, and a denial of, Jewish life in the diaspora. In his argument, he describes pre-Zionist or diasporic Jewish life as a world of darkness, paradox, and negation. Sorrow replaces happiness as an ideal and pain becomes the norm rather than pleasure; there is tearing down rather than building up, slavery rather than redemption, dream rather than reality, vague hope rather than real plans, faith rather than common sense—and so on and so forth, one paradox after another. "[I]t's simply dreadful! A different psychology comes into being, a psychology of the night . . . You see, there is a psychology of the night which differs from that of the day. Not the psychology of a man in the night—that's something else; a psychology of the night itself."[11]

This is an accurate description of the world depicted in such stories as "A Blessed Fall Dawn," "Christians," "Hanale," and "The Gift." A world of unbearable suffering which results in an aesthetic response in the form of these literary stories, a difficult, dark—and to use Hazaz's metaphor—nocturnal ideal. This could not be further removed from the experience, and the expression in Hebrew literature, of the socialist-Zionist political and cultural project of state-building.

The landscape of Palestine, with its barren hills, scorching summers, and stormy winters, and the Modern Hebrew of its first Zionist settlers, still harsh and new on their lips, was demanding in its brazen realism, harsh truths, and

---

10   *Hagana* (lit. The Defence) was the main Zionist paramiltary organization of the Jewish population (*Yishuv*) in Mandatory Palestine between 1920 and its disestablishment in 1948, when it became the core of the Israel Defence Forces (IDF).

11   Haim Hazaz, "The Sermon" [trans. Hillel Halkin], in *The Sermon And Other Stories* (New Milford, CT: The Toby Press, 2005), 238.

programmatic diction. There was no room under the bright Israeli sun and in Hebrew prose for the mysterious, the uncanny, the gothic. For Hebrew readers in 1920s Palestine, and to a great extant until today, the unnatural and the horror of recurring deaths belonged in the dark woods of Europe and in its foreign literature. Hameiri is unique is bringing the European gothic, the diaspora Jewish identity, and the visionary-pioneering Zionist worldview together. He is all of them and while these different worlds do not sit comfortably in his stories, his work does not aim to comfort, it is there to document; his wartime stories are a memorial, but also a warning.

In his introduction to *The Great Madness*, Hameiri states that "I had not set out to observe the Jew in myself and in my comrades-in-death, but that is how it turned out."[12] The Jewish protagonists in his stories represent a wide and varied Jewish European world. The pious Hasidic Jew is worlds away from the emancipated and sometimes assimilated Jewish scientist, and yet Hameiri identifies that which links them, and this allusive Jewish identity becomes his theme as well as his motivation for writing. This is evident in his poetry too, and in the selection presented here, where the speaker has a personal "I" and yet is also an "everyman" or, rather, an "everyJew."

However, despite the total commitment to and empathy for the very differing experiences of the Jews of Europe due to the violence of the Great War, Hameiri still writes of the human experience. The stories and poems are ultimately a study of the horror of war suffered by the survivor. While death is all around, those who survive do not truly experience it, and cannot describe it. The worst experience of the survivor is the fear of death. Hameiri writes: "No artist in the world has the power to describe even a thousandth of what is known to you as the fear of death."[13] Acknowledging the limitation of language to do so, Hameiri nonetheless dedicates his pen to do exactly that. This anthology is the only example of a Modern Hebrew writer whose work is about the nightmarish world of a constant and very real fear of death. By committing to paper these tales of extreme pain, fear, and despair, Hameiri gives voice to lost lives and the unspoken vulnerability of the European Jewish experience.

—*Tamar S. Drukker*

---

12   Hameiri, *The Great Madness*, 47.

13   See 114-129, 167. To be inserted with galleys.

Avigdor Hameiri

War Stories and Poetry

Under a Bloodred Sky[1]

Come to me now and caress—
In vain, youth's song has dried:
Here do I stand, my pale beauty,
under a bloodred sky.

Come to me now and taunt me—
In vain, here all eyes are blind:
I am occupied here, my pale beauty,
within me millions die.

Come to me now, soft as dew—
In vain, I shall not embrace:
I tread your winepress, my pale beauty,
lest I defile your faded grace.

Come to me now and admonish—
In vain, sanity has escaped my mind;
Here I stand, my pale beauty,
under a bloodred sky.

---

1   Avigdor Feuerstein, "Tahat Shamaim Adumim," in *Masu'ot: Collections Dedicated to the Questions of the Times, Studies and Literature*, ed. Moshe Glickson (Odessa: Omanut Publishing, 1919), 330.

Christians (or, How My Hair Turned White Overnight)[1]

> "The Creator of the Universe is the greatest fantasist."

> *(my grandfather)*

How many of you have had the pleasure of seeing your own grave being dug?

The war granted me this great honor, during one night as a Russian prisoner of war.

We were sent to the enemy front as scouts. Of the five of us, it just so happened that three were Jews and two non-Jews. I myself don't like this distinction into "Jew and non-Jew" at all, but the events I am describing didn't ask my opinion: fate forced it upon me. I have been compelled to feel my Jewishness—to an atrocious degree.

Let me begin. Our group consisted of three Jews and two Magyars. We had already been able to bring back valuable information from the Russian lines. But suddenly—we fell into their trap and were taken captive. Enemy scouts surrounded us on all sides. There was no escape—we had been captured. It was 10:00 pm.

Our captors, thirty in number, led us to a small, half-destroyed village. One of us, a Magyar, escaped back to our lines, so only four of us could be taken to their commander. They searched us more strictly than the most Orthodox of Jews examines his house for hametz on Pesach eve.[2] They even

---

1   Avigdor Feuerstein, "Notzrim," *Hatekufa* 14-15, Tevet-Sivan Tarpav (1922), 85-97. This story is summarized in Avigdor Hameiri, *The Great Madness*, ed. Peter C. Appelbaum (Middletown, RI: Stone Tower Press and Boston, Ma: Black Widow Press, 2021), 232-238.

2   The night before Pesach, immediately after sundown, the search for leaven (*bedikat hametz*) begins. The aim of the search is to be sure that no leaven has been left behind after the cleaning of the house. The next morning it is ceremonially burned (*bi'ur hametz*).

removed our pocket handkerchiefs. Everything we owned was like leaven before Pesach in their eyes, to be removed. They brought us before their senior officer stripped of all possessions. Our destination was a small, dilapidated hut, covered with rotten straw, which resembled a typical Galician plebeian dwelling. It's hat, that is to say its roof, was turned to the side and one of its ears peeped out of a hole in the dusty attic. Its two dark, half-opened eyes—the windows—blinked at us with naked, unrestrained loathing. The hate of a beggar on horseback reflected at us from it. The sounds of rowdy, drunken laughter and singing reverberated from the hut. We recognized it instantly. This was the Russian command post.

They forced us into the drunken hut. As soon as the door was opened, we were hit by a stream of hot, stifling air and an asphyxiating stench of brandy mixed with smoke. It was as if the hut opened its evil maw and breathed out it's filthy, drunken lungs, which blinded the eye, deafened the ear, and defiled the soul.

A wild scene unfolded before our eyes. A set table full of bottles and glasses standing in a puddle of spilled, stinking liquor of all colors. Soldiers, officers, and various other Russians stood around the table: infantrymen, cavalrymen, Cossacks, and just plain drunkards—smoking, drinking, half out of their mind with inebriated rowdiness. The Russian Unteroffizier[3] who led us here stood before one of them, informing him respectfully that he had brought in some Austrian prisoners. The officer, nearly insensible with liquor, looked at us with fogged-up eyes and said as if understanding what was happening: "Good. Make yourself scarce." He didn't even look at us or take note of our lowly existence: he sang to himself and drank and drank. One of the men sitting behind him started to bellow a Jewish song, which didn't disturb the others. After all, they knew nothing about harmony, and continued to bellow their own songs in noisy cacophony.

I looked around me. The walls were filled with holy icons overgrown with spiders' webs which had been almost torn away with dust. A kind of officer lay sprawled on the bed snoring from the depths of his nose in time with the hellish bellowing around him. Pieces of pork roasting in their own fat sizzled in the fire on the stove, their smell mixing with the stench of smoke and liquor to create a nauseating hellish odor. A man lay under the table without moving. I looked carefully—he didn't have a head.

---

3   In Austro-Hungarian parlance, noncommissioned officer.

My entire body shook violently. The drunkenness which at first astonished me ceased to be important and I looked at my friends wordlessly.

"Where is the head?"

We found it standing upright on the table between the many bottles and glasses, in a puddle of red wine. Its eyed were half open, a smoldering cigar in its mouth.

It wasn't difficult to recognize that this was the head of a Jew. Only he who speaks the language of demons and foul spirits can find the words to describe the feelings that welled up in me at this sight. The sight of dead bodies, amputated limbs, wounds, body parts are the commonplace of a war that is fought for uprightness and freedom. But this was a little more than uprightness and a call for freedom—it was an abomination.

These are my thoughts now, writing about the event after the fact. But at the time I had no thoughts at all. The mixture of smoke and cigars, the stench of liquor mixed with warm human blood, made everything so indistinct that my brain couldn't function. My eyes started to wobble, my heart pounded and rose into my throat, my saliva became sour, and visions of hell arose in my brain.

The officer's voice awoke me from the fog of tumult:

"Who is the senior ranking officer?"

I swallowed my revulsion and my head began to spin.

"I am."

"Are you a Jew?"

"Yes."

"Very good. Are there any other Jews in your group?"

"I am," one of my comrades said.

"I can see that from the sly expression on your face. Anyone else?"

"I am," a second comrade said in a trembling, colorless voice.

"You are all Jews! Hell and damnation! A gang of Jews! Are you a Jew too?" He asked one of the Magyars.

"Me? No."

"Nu: three Jews. Very good!"

"Excellent!" a second officer said. "They've come at the right time. By my life, the right time!"

"Do you Jews know what today is?"

I remembered that today was the Russian Orthodox Christmas, but said nothing.[4] The officer added:

"Today is a very important and holy day for us, Jews; the birthday of the Son of God. Do you know what that means?"

"Yes," we all answered drily.

"Good. Of course you know. You should know it even better than we Christians, because this day came to redeem you as well. You assisted the Messiah in purifying us from all our sins and transgressions by his agony on the cross. Therefore, as thanks, you will celebrate Christmas with us. Where are you from, Jews?"

"From Hungary."

"Hungary? Ah, yes, I believe I have heard that Hungarian Jews are experts in this. Tell me, Jews, is it true that Hungarian Jews are experts in drinking Christian blood?"

We stood in silent astonishment. What could we possibly say?

"Well, why do you remain silent? It's an open secret." He turned to me: "Please tell me. As the senior ranking officer, you must know more than the others. Exactly how do the Jews drink Christian blood?"

It was as if my saliva turned into sour pus. I swallowed again and remained silent. He continued:

"You too? Why do you also remain silent? It isn't seemly. How can you possibly remain silent?" He turned to the Magyar: "The Jews remain silent, but surely you know. How do Hungarian Jews drink Christian blood? How do they drink your blood?"

The Magyar stood correctly to attention, coughed, and said:

"Herr Commandant, our Jews do not drink Christian blood. There are no cannibals amongst us."

The officer shook his head.

"What is your religion?" He asked in amazement. "Are you a Christian?"

"Yes."

"So? As a member of the Christian faith, do you hide the sins of the Jews? Or are you afraid of them?"

"No."

---

4   Because the Eastern Orthodox Church follows the Julian calendar, their Christmas falls on 7 January.

"Obviously. You have nothing to fear from them now. They can do you no harm here Don't be afraid: tell me everything you know . . ."

The Magyar looked at me and said nothing. But the way he looked at me gave me a bad feeling, because it looked as though he was afraid of me. I turned to him and said:

"Tell him, Andras. Tell him what you know."

The Magyar who, up till now, had stood at attention facing the Russian officer, made a proper, sharp turn, faced me, and said in Hungarian, with a hard but confident voice:

"Sir! I say nothing! I will not lie for that pig!"

The officer was filled with anger because the Magyar was speaking to me and not to him. I told the Magyar to address the Russian and not me, but he didn't move, saying with a reddened face:

"What should I say to that revolting pig?"

The Russian officer rose angrily and berated him with gritted teeth. The Magyar moved, faced the officer, and said in broken Russian Ukrainian:

"I will not lie! I am a Magyar!"

He emphasized these words in so harsh a voice that the Russian was taken aback and did not reply. He smiled mockingly, turned to me, and said:

"You really play your tricks excellently. You obstruct and educate your own animals most expertly. So, you don't want to admit the truth like an honest man?"

The situation was clear to me. I came to my senses and said:

"Officer, sir. It's obvious that you know the answers to all these questions, just as I do. You're an officer, an educated man. I am also an officer and cannot be untrue to myself. We are all in your hands to do with as you see fit. We are after all your captives . . ."

The Russian burst out laughing:

"Ha! You can't be untrue to yourself? Ha! A member of the race of Judas Iscariot can't tell a lie? That's really rich! A Jew can't tell a lie! That's really interesting! We'll soon see!"

He poured drinks for himself and his comrades and they all drank. Then one the officers addressed the head on the table:

"Nu, yid, what do you say about your brethren? All loyal Jews, isn't that so? They don't reveal their secrets. They are just as silent as you are, yid."

They all burst out in wild laughter.

"Yes," a third said, "this Jew has been completely silenced: he will never lie again, nor reveal any more secrets. We need to light his cigar again; its light has gone out. Give me a match."

A Cossack with squashed nose and small ratty eyes lit the cold cigar. The ignited flame singed the hair and moustache on the old man's head and the officer poured a glass of wine over it.

We closed our eyes at this horrible sight and turned our heads to the wall. My saliva dried up: there was nothing to swallow. I felt as if thin needles had been stuck diagonally into my throat and my heart sank into my boots. I leaned against the wall and felt a heavy load on my shoulder—my friend was leaning on me. The wall was damp, cold, and pleasant. For a moment I felt that I wanted to vomit. Then the pleasant sounds of a bell. The clock on the wall chimed: 8, 9,10, 13, 20, 32—infinity. I stopped counting. Let it ring. Wild laughter— "Curl the moustache!" "Beautiful!"—"What a handsome Jew!"

A horrifying voice brought me back to reality:

"What about dinner, boys?"

"At once, sir!"

I opened my eyes. The soldier at the stove handed out the roasted pork to all those seated at the table and they started to eat.

The officer turned to me: "Sit down until we finish our meal."

We sat on the long couch situated behind us. Just in time—I stood unsteadily, like a drunken man. I felt my blood descending from my brain to my legs, which were too tired to carry me anymore. Not one of my comrades looked at the table: they sat with closed eyes. The head with the cigar in its mouth was soaked with spilled wine. I felt nauseated again: my stomach convulsed. "We have to feed the yid as well." "Open his mouth and fatten him up." "He is our guest today." "Take the cigar out." "But he doesn't have a belly!" "Ha!" A hammer beat in my brain. I leaned in a corner. Good. But I still felt the hammer: it beat and beat: "Ha." I heard a strange voice in the distance: a soft, imploring voice: "What do you want of me?" "I am just a simple Jew."—"I am a Jew." "I have small sons." The body under the table began to twitch and real tears trickled from the head's eyes . . . A whitish, pure, transparent mist hovered over the smoke in the house . . . like a soul beating its wings . . . like a bird over the head of a cat eating its chick.

A cruel reprimand frightened me:

"Get up, Jews! This isn't a time to sleep! It's a sacred holiday!"

We got up. The Magyar got up as well.

"You can sit down," said the officer. "You aren't a Jew."

The Magyar stood with us.

"Sit down, I told you!"

The Magyar remained where he was.

"Durak![5] Idiot!" The officer turned to his friends. "Stupid Magyar!"

"Sit down," I said to him, "sit down, Andras."

The officer boiled over with rage. He came up to me, his nose almost touching my face, mouth emitting foul liquor fumes, eyes almost bulging out of their sockets:

"Shut up, you son of a bitch! God-cursed Jew! I'll teach you to give orders here!" He turned to one of his friends: "Alexei Fyodorovich, what do you think? Which one of them should we start with?"

"This one," he said, pointing to one of my comrades. "He is a typical Jew. Look at his nose and eyes—typically Jewish. He has the beak of a ravening vulture! Ha!"

He laughed and dropped onto the sofa, drunk as a skunk.

"What's your name?"

"Avraham—Avra—." The Russian interrupted him:

"No need to say more. Avraham is enough. Nu, Avraham—listen. Listen, all of you. This officer's court martial has been appointed to judge you. Your guilt is well known to all. By majority vote, we have decided to do to you as you have done to us. Firstly, because you drink Christian blood, one of you will have to drink Jewish blood. Secondly, because you crucified the Son of God, one of you will be crucified. Thirdly, one of you will be buried alive, like the Son of God who was buried but rose from the grave. Do you understand?" He turned back to the table, clinked glasses with his comrades, and they all drank. Then he turned to us again:

"You, Avraham will drink Jewish blood. What do you say to that? You remain silent? You still have permission to speak.'

"..."

The officer smiled.

"We are not the one sitting in judgment over you. No: the real Judge sits on high and you can all be satisfied with His decision. After all, He too was

---

5   Fool (Russian).

a Jew once: Jesus of Nazareth the Son of Man. He was a rabbi: Jesus the son of Joseph. And so, in the name of Rabbi Jesus of Nazareth—bring the blood!"[6]

One of them gave Avraham a glass full of what looked like red wine. When he handed it to him, I saw that it was congealed blood mixed with wine. He pushed it under Avraham's mouth. I smelt the blood stench: Avraham recoiled, raising his hand to his mouth. His eyes became alive and he smiled. He didn't believe what was happening.

The officer snarled at him:

"What? You're smiling? You're laughing, you God-cursed Jew? Drink, you son of a bitch!" Avraham turned his face aside and the officer's anger seemed to evaporate somewhat.

"Don't you want it?" he said in a quiet voice. "Drink, drink. It's kosher Jewish blood, after all."

I thought that he was poking fun at him. I don't know how and why, but a smile came over my face as well. The officer turned to me:

"Are you also smiling? We'll soon see, how you fulfil your duty!" . . . Nu, Avraham, I order you to drink up this glass of blood immediately!"

He took out a revolver with his other hand, raised it to Avraham's head, and said:

"I order you to drink up this glass of blood immediately. If you don't, this will be your grave!"

" . . ."

"Take him!" the Russian commanded his comrade. "Tie him up!"

One of them grabbed Avraham, tied his hands behind him with a strap, and bent his head upwards. Another pushed the cup onto his clenched mouth . . .

"Open your damned mouth!" ordered the senior officer. He took a bayonet off one of the rifles and forced Avraham's mouth open with it. The bayonet entered easily. The poor man didn't feel anything anymore because he fainted and fell over. They put him on the floor with the bayonet in his mouth against his clenched teeth. The officer put his leg on Avraham's chest, twisting the bayonet to and fro inside his mouth. The bayonet grated against the teeth, breaking several of them but the mouth didn't open. They took

---

6   This paragraph does not appear in the original version, but in Avigdor Hameiri, *Sipu-rei Milhama* (Tel Aviv: Am Oved, 1970), 170. In the 1970 edition, the story is entitled "In the Name of Rabbi Jesus of Nazareth."

a second bayonet, stuck it in, and finally managed to prize the poor man's mouth open. The officer poured the red blood mixture into the open mouth: it went in and some dribbled out, but Avraham didn't move. His face turned bluish white, the blood mixture dripped onto both cheeks, but he still didn't move. My head began to spin, I felt the salty taste of blood on my tongue, my heart stopped beating, and I couldn't take my eyes off Avraham's face—they looked and looked at him . . . I tried to clench them shut but it was impossible. They looked and looked. Was he dead? Suddenly his body twitched terribly, like a cow after slaughter. His face convulsed backwards behind his neck and a horrible shower of blood shot up from his mouth, followed by projectile vomit of yellow, blue-green, red, and white material. The vomit dripped back onto his face. He vomited again—this time all over the officer's face. His body became pale, twitched again, and sprawled on the ground, legs trembling, head lolling to the side . . . finally, eternal rest came to the tortured man.

"Miserable son of a bitch!" the officer exploded angrily, wiping the filth from his face. "Get him out of here! Throw him to the side!"

They took the dead body and hurled it against the wall. The officer wet his face with eau de cologne, drank a glass of brandy, and turned to his friends who had witnessed the proceedings with drunken eyes. They laughed, commented about it, and drank some more. "It's about time these damned Jews drank some Jewish blood: they only drink Christian blood." That son of a bitch!" "Who will be next?" asked the officer without any outward signs of excitement, after drinking some more. "Whom should we crucify?"

"Their senior ranking officer." One pointed to me.

A word formed on my lips, but I swallowed it. Beads of sweat dropped from my brow, ears, head, and hair.

"No," one of them said, "the one with the most senior rank must be buried alive. He will be resurrected from the dead."

Again a word started to burst from my mouth; again I choked it off.

"So, this one will be next" the officer said, pointing to another of my comrades. "What is your name?"

Silence.

"What is your name you bastard?"

Silence.

"Nothing? Nu, so we'll call you Judas Iscariot. Yes, Judas Iscariot. You will be crucified, like your forefathers crucified the Son of God!"

I looked at my comrade's wet, damp face. A burning stream stabbed me through the heart and my eyes filled with tears. I didn't stop them: let the tears flow, let them drown and blind my eyes, let my eyes pour out their contents. Why should they be able to see?

When two men approached to tie my second comrade up, he recoiled, pressed his body to mine, and embraced me so tightly that he almost squeezed my breath out. I thought to myself: "Let me choke and die rather than see this," and embraced him as well.

They separated us, pushed me to the side, took hold of his two hands, and led him to the wall on which two holy icons hung: one of the Virgin Mary with the baby Jesus, the other of the crucified Christ. They removed the icons. Hammers, nails, and other implements were bought in. The poor man's whole body shook and he burst out into terrible weeping: loud, moaning weeping without saying a word, like a little boy whose cruel teacher takes his belt off prior to beating him black and blue. He cried without words. The Magyar standing at his side made a movement towards him.

"Why are you bellowing?" he called out in a loud, rasping voice, tender and full of compassion and love at the same time. "Why are you bellowing like an ox? Christ the Messiah is looking: he sees all of this and he won't forget. At least bash the senior officer in his disgusting snout first, and then you can let them do what they want to do to you! But do something!"

The poor man turned to us and wept uncontrollably, imploring us to help him:

"What do they want?" he moaned, choking in tears. "What do they want from me? What do they w-a-n-t?"

The Magyar couldn't stand it anymore. He reached out to him with one hand and pressed his hand, putting the other on his shoulder:

"Don't cry, my friend. Don't cry," he said in a voice filled with compassion. "Don't cry!" he said in an even louder voice. He gritted his teeth, balled his one fist like iron, and looked at the Russian officer with a poisonous glare. He went up to the holy icons lying on a crate, raised his fist to them, and said in a choking, tear-filled voice:

"Christ, seven times holy Son of God, you foul bastard! Look, O Messiah!"

The officer beat him and shoved him aside:

"Ha, Magyar, you wild animal! I'll teach you a lesson! You'll follow your Jews into hell! Bind his hands and feet together!"

The Magyar didn't pay attention to what he was saying. He went up to his poor friend again, shook his hand fiercely and warmly, looked deeply into his eyes, embraced him like a brother, looked at him again, and said:

"The Lord will be with you.[7] Don't be afraid. Show these pigs how bravely a Jew can die."

I too went up to my friend, but didn't have the strength to shake his hand. They pushed us aside. I said something to him in a choked and tearful voice that I myself didn't hear, and we returned to our places.

Those miserable curs then set down a stool next to the wall and put the Jew on it. They raised his two hands to the side, took a long nail, and thrust it into his one hand. I didn't close my eyes but looked and looked. The poor man didn't say a word, but bit his lower lip and grimaced. They drove the nail in with a kind of axe. He began to take long, deep breaths, and whistled like a broken flute. They struck and struck, driving the nail into the wall. They continued drinking. One of them looked behind him and said: "That's it, that's it, boys." One of the officers went outside. "I'll return very soon" he said. Red blood dripped from his one hand. A second officer went outside as well. I turned my head to the side and continued to look—I looked and looked. They drove another nail into his other hand and the poor man let out a long, deep, weak, trembling sound like a crying dog. The voice broke into pieces. He bellowed, twisted his head to the side, and looked at us. Oh, his eyes! His eyes! He closed them and I felt a terrible pain. Where? I felt an excruciating pain in my palm. No, in my palate, in the pit of my heart . . . The crucified man's head collapsed to the side. A reddish-black curtain descended on my brain. The hammer struck and struck and struck . . .

A sudden, horrible yell resounded. The poor wretch tore himself from the wall, attacking the Russians with wild and terrible force. He struck them blindly right and left, with his hands and legs, butted and kicked like an enraged bull. They tried, but couldn't pin him down. He hit, rammed, swept away, kicked, slapped, pushed—he snatched up the axe from one of them and swung it right and left, hitting all in its path. The Russians were terrified and pushed at him from all sides. "Catch him! Catch him!" the officer cried, cursing, blood dripping from his head and hand. One Russian lay on the floor with a wound in his head. The Magyar jumped, up and down, crying: "Kill them! Kill them! Comrade! Kill them! Aha! Good! Kill them! Cut them down!" He

---

7   The Magyar uses a Jewish euphemism for God (The Name). See note 11.

rubbed his hands, screaming with mad, victorious, teeth-gnashing glee. The wounded Jew jerked like a wild animal who had been set free and kept on hitting out blindly at men, bottles, even air. After they finally caught him again, he fell on the ground on our dead comrade, bellowed like a felled ox, and fell silent. A bloody froth came out of his mouth. The officer took out the revolver from his pocket and shot him in the head three times. He stuck the gun in our faces, his hand weak and trembling. He approached us and said, calmly without anger and somewhat hoarsely, his head and hands dripping blood:

"No. No. I won't kill you. Do you see this blood?" He pointed to the blood dripping from his head. "I won't kill you. I'll bury you all alive. And not both of you together. You!" he turned to my Magyar comrade. "You will stand and watch, then it will be your turn. Catch them!"

But the officers were occupied with themselves. One bound up the officer's wounded head with lint. They all drank and cursed, cursed and drank. They swore in low voices, astonished at the Jew's strength, against which they couldn't stand.

"He went mad," said one as if justifying himself. "He went out of his mind. Were it not for that, we could easily have overcome him." He sprawled on the couch. "We must tie these two up properly, so that they don't go mad as well."

"They won't become mad again," the officer said. "I—I will show them. I'll teach them decent manners. Tie them up tightly!"

They tied us up: we didn't fight against it. The strap and thin rope cut into my hands. We both stood, hands tied behind us. I felt neither pain nor fear, but I felt hot, very hot, and sweated.

The officer went up to my comrade the Magyar:

"Shame and disgrace!" he said to him. "Aren't you ashamed of yourself? You are a Christian!"

The Magyar gritted his teeth, stood up straight, and said, in a voice full of certainty and contempt:

"You are wrong! I'm not a Christian! I'm a Jew as well! Do to me what you want to do with my Herr Offizier! I too am a Jew!"

I looked at him. Had I not known otherwise, I really would have thought that he was a Jew. I wanted to tell him something—but had no strength to speak. I wanted to embrace him—but my hands were tied.

"Nu, if you really are a Jew," the officer said, "you will be sentenced like a Jew!" His eyes glowed like the fires of hell.

He turned to his men and said:

"Boys, go dig the graves!"

The men went.

One of the officers suddenly rose and said:

"Leave these sons of bitches! Let them go to hell! Shoot them—put a bullet in their brains! I'm sick of them already!"

"What?" The officer got angry. "Shoot them? Look at this blood!"—he pointed to his head. "What about it? No, my friend, you are wrong. I'll bury them alive—alive, I tell you!"

Silence. They rearranged the upper table and drank some more, tired and silent. The head on the table was pushed onto the side. The exposed severed windpipe and esophagus made my blood run cold and my body trembled. We heard the heavy, dead thudding of earth clods thrown against the walls of the hut. We stood there not looking at one another. As I remember it, the Magyar asked me: "Is it really true that they are going to bury us alive?" More dull thuds. Then silence—silence, heavy as lead. The officer wandered back and forth, drunk as a skunk. The wall clock rang: one—the sound entered my brain and sang—din-din-din-din. A pleasant warmth came over me—a feeling of drunkenness. Now more than ever seems it rich to die, to fall asleep while sitting, to fall into a dreamless sleep, without feeling anything. The warmth in my heart's blood shrank and my heart stopped beating. My soul drifted like warm vapor, dissipating from me like a pleasant odor. I lay underground, under the earth, my soul rose from the heavy material and rose up to heaven. My mother was there, waiting for her son's soul. She welcomed me with sad compassion, gave me a warm, healing, motherly, tearful kiss, and lulled me to sleep on her knees.[8] I sat on her lap embracing her warm, dear, caring, rejuvenating body, and purified myself before her. They beat me, tortured me,[9] buried me alive. I pressed her to me, buried my head in her bosom, and slept—perchance to dream? My two dead friends rose from the dead . . . They smiled: It was terrible, wasn't it? But nevertheless we're alive—they didn't succeed!" They laughed with joy and went wild, like cherubs, like children. Joy, happiness, brightness, song—din, din, din—

A coarse, terrifying voice awoke my reverie.

"Nu, dogs, come with me!"

---

8   Hameiri's mother died when he was a young boy.

9   After Isaiah 53:7.

We went outside. It was a cold night, damp and full of thick mist. The grave was almost finished: they dug and dug. One had a candle in his hand. "Deeper, deeper!" the officer ordered. My Magyar friend stood silently, looking into the grave. Suddenly, he turned to me:

"Brother," he said in a strange voice. "Brother! Recite a Jewish prayer with me—a Hebrew prayer: Brother!"

"Brother"—that word came from another world.[10] "Brother" is the warmest, dearest word in the Hungarian language. It signifies humble, domestic, love without obligation or etiquette. "Brother" is a shared prayer in the face of hopeless danger. If a soldier forgets his own character and the fear of his superior to such a degree that he cries out "Brother"—that in itself signifies terrible death. The Magyar said to me: "Brother, please pray with me in Hebrew."

"No need, my good friend, no need. You are a Christian—pray to your God. The same maker created us."

The Magyar stood up straight.

"Who?" he said almost angrily. "I am a Christian? I? With these impure beasts? With that bastard?"

His voice became imploring.

"Please—do this for me—teach me a short Hebrew prayer. Teach me the name of your God."

"His name? I don't know it. He has no name . . ."[11]

"What prayer? I know: I remember that I found one of your prayers once: 'Adonai.' Please—'Adonai.'"

At that moment, the thick curtain fell from my soul and my body sprouted wings. My heart began to beat lightly, singingly, blessedly, playing, playing, playing.

I bent over my friend's face and, hands tied behind me, gave him a warm kiss. He kissed me back. His kiss was full of warmth, sweetness, sorrow mixed with happiness and the pain of eternal pleasure.

---

10 The Hungarian for brother is *testver* (*test*, body; *vér*, blood).

11 This is an extremely complex issue. For the ultra-Orthodox, God has more than eighty names. The real name of God, *hashem hameforash*, was only known to the high priest, and was forgotten in time after the destruction of the Second Temple in 70 CE. While praying, God is usually referred to as Elohim or Adonai. The tetragrammaton is the written Hebrew name of God, transliterated in four letters as *YHWH* or *JHVH* and articulated by non-Jews as Yahweh or Jehovah, is read as Adonai and may only be articulated reverently, during prayer. During lay conversation, God is referred to as Hashem (The Name).

I said to him:

"Andras, say after me: Shema—'Shema,' Yisrael—'Yisrael,' Adonai— 'Adonai,' Eloheinu—'Eloheinu,' Adonai—'Adonai,' Ehad—'Ehad.'[12] Now say Yitgadal—'Yitgadal,' Veyitkadash—'Veyitkadash,' Shmei—'Shmei,' Rabbah— 'rabbah,' bealm—"[13] Suddenly, a shot rang out from a distance, cutting through the mist—za-za-a-a-a-a!!! A huge shell exploded near us, then another shot, and another—one-two-three-four, followed by many more, one after the other, all exploded very near where we were standing—rapidly, quickly. Our blood began to boil and I felt new life coursing through my body, limbs, heart, and brain. My heart pounded loudly. The firing drew nearer and nearer, un-ceasing, the roar became an earsplitting tumult. The two gravediggers pushed, shoved, and ran around terrified. "Sirs! Sirs" the gravediggers called: *"Pani! Pani!*[14] Come here! Jump in!" We jumped into the pit, between the gravedig-gers. They welcomed us lovingly—they actually caressed us. "It doesn't matter, sirs, it doesn't matter! Very good! Very good!" They untied our hands. The bombardment became even more ferocious, the hut burned, and the sound of drunken wailing was heard inside it. One of the diggers embraced me and cursed the officer who had ordered him to dig the grave. He pushed a pick into my hands, the other gave my friend a rifle with bayonet attached. "Don't think badly of us, sirs, we aren't guilty. He is our enemy, not our friend. Don't think badly of the two of us!" Dying wailing and screamed commands were heard from the hut. One of the officers wanted to jump into the pit with us—it was his only refuge. The Magyar thrust his bayonet into him with terrible anger. "Take that!" one of the Russian gravediggers said. "Take that, you filthy son of a bitch!" The bombardment added to the mountain of fire in the destroyed hut, but then moved away from us, following the fleeing Russians. The shells flew above our heads, exploding far away. There were no enemy soldiers left around us.

Shells were exploding on the fleeing Russians, so it wasn't dangerous to climb out of the pit. Our soldiers arrived and I ran as fast as I could towards them in the snow. I heard a voice behind me: "Sir! Sir! Wait a bit!" I looked—it

---

12 The Jewish confession of faith, recited just before death. "Hear, O Israel, the Lord our God, the Lord is One."

13 The beginning of the mourner's kaddish: "Glorified and sanctified be God's great name throughout the world . . ."

14 Sirs (Russian).

was the Magyar walking towards me, rifle slung over his shoulder, its bayonet thrust into a corpse, torn almost in half.

"Here it is, sir!" he said happily, purring like a cat playing with a dead mouse. "Here it is . . . a Christian!"

He threw the body onto the snow, stuck the bayonet into it again once, twice, three times . . . I lit a match: his head looked as though it was covered with flour. His hair had gone snow white—he had become old overnight. "What has happened to you?" I asked. "You look the same way," he answered. He turned towards the body in the snow and thrust his bayonet into its belly one more time with a furious roar. I looked at the dead man's face.

"The officer."

Silence[1]

The sun is red. It's laid to bed.
Here I lie.
Silence.

I raise my eyes with dread.
Above me ravens spread.
Silence.

A red maggot in my head.
It sleeps. It has been fed.
Silence.

The sun is red. It's laid to bed.
Here I lie.
Silence.

---

1   Avigdor Hameiri, "Silence," *Sefer Ha'shirim* (Tel Aviv: Am Ha'sefer, 1933), 232.

Revenge[1]

For Herman Jadlowker[2]

1.

The reservists who arrive in our trenches today include my young, dearly be-loved friend Freidi. Freidi is a young officer of about twenty with a baby face and eyes that look into the soul rather than into the colorful world around him. I have known him for more than three years. The first time we met, he was playing the violin, serving as music's bridegroom during a soaring concert. At the age of only fifteen, he was already praised as a significant new artist. More than the content of his playing, people were astonished at his amazingly sophisticated technique for one so young. He played with the insight and ma-turity of an old man with sixty to seventy seasons under his belt. Freidi was looked on as a young virtuoso with sublime promise, whose renown would surely spread from his homeland to the entire world.

In Budapest,[3] Freidi was the youngest member of our merry band of Gyp-sy night owls who, together, immersed ourselves in love for that well-known harlot, known during the day as "art." But for us it was modest and domesti-cated, if a little tipsy and sad to the point of suicide for the sake of the world to come. In that group we listened to Freidi with a different ear, different from ears which would listen to him outside our domain, in noisy concerts exuding the perfume of dolled-up women and well-to-do men with pressed, counter-feit hearts.

---

1   Avigdor Feuerstein, "Nekama," *Hatekufa*, Tamuz-Elul, Tarpah (1921), 89-99.

2   Herman Jadlowker (1877-1953), leading Latvian-born tenor of Russian (later Israeli) nationality, who enjoyed an important international career during the first quarter of the twentieth century.

3   Hameiri refers to it as "the city."

It was impossible to put Freidi's art into words. There was something strange about it which could not be described or dissected out with a scalpel. A perception that couldn't be described in word or thought, but which became clearer and clearer to every member of our group. We didn't speak about it, some out of politeness, others simply didn't attach any importance to it. But we all felt it nevertheless. *Freidi played the violin in a Jewish style*, although he wasn't Jewish. In our group, this question was of no importance at all—Jew or non-Jew, we couldn't have cared less. We all felt beyond this level of distinction between art and language, how much more so between different religions. Surely art is universal and belongs to all mankind! This is especially so with music.

But this style—if I am permitted to call it that—was quite stubborn. It kept evolving, becoming more and more prominent. It almost became an essential part of his playing style. As if to irritate people, Freidi became "Mr. Perfect in everything that he played."[4] It made no difference whether it was Meyerbeer or Beethoven, Grieg or Bach, Schumann or Puccini—everything was played in a Jewish style.[5]

We would never have spoken of this amongst ourselves. But once an actress in our group innocently brought up a certain sonata which she didn't recognize when Freidi played it. It had to be a Jewish melody, didn't it? We answered her jestingly that she was exceptionally foolish: it was a sonata by Liszt.[6] Hearing this, Freidi's whole body started to tremble. His face became pale and with one movement he threw his violin down with a curse. At that moment, I felt that we couldn't carry on like this and we had to "set the record straight," because it went to the heart of Freidi's honor. Not because of contempt for the Jews, but because the sonata had nothing to do with them and this false accusation was an abomination, slandering him by accusing him of playing it in an inappropriate style.

---

4   Sarcastic modern Hebrew expression—"a completely blue tallit"; widely used to refer to something that is ostensibly, but not really, absolutely pure, immaculate, and virtuous.

5   Giacomo Meyerbeer (Jacob Liebmann Beer) (1791-1864), German born composer of French grand opera; Ludwig van Beethoven (1770-1827), German composer and pianist; Edvard Grieg (1843-1907), Norwegian composer and pianist; Johann Sebastian Bach (1685-1750), German composer and musician of the baroque period; Robert Schumann (1810-1856), German composer, pianist, and influential music critic; Giacomo Puccini (1858-1924), Italian opera composer.

6   Franz Liszt (1811-1886), Hungarian pianist and composer.

I, as one who loved him and was loved in return, struck up a conversation about the matter. As if by accident he started to speak about it, in a negative way and with great objection.

"This is unexampled stupidity," he said angrily. "Absolutely preposterous!"

"No, Freidi, not at all. There is much truth in it. There are issues that have no relevance to Jewish music, or Jewish life in general: you give them Jewish color and Jewish content."

"Maybe it's simply an eastern influence?"

"Eastern? Even if it is, does it make any real difference? The main thing, Freidi, is that . . ."

"True," he admitted, "it really is the same thing. To play Liszt's Sixth Hungarian Rhapsody or Beethoven's *Moonlight* Sonata in Jewish, or maybe just eastern style, is certainly an inner sickness. But what can I do about it?" he asked with deeply touching, innocent, child-like sadness.

"What can you do? Nothing, Freidi. 'If I am for myself, what am I?'"[7] I added with emphasis: "In your place, I wouldn't make too much of a fuss over it. It isn't an unheard-of thing and maybe it's only temporary, dependent on time, place, or something else. They said about Joachim that, in his youth, every melody he played—even the most cheerful—was full of cursed, poison-filled devilish laughter.[8] It's no great tragedy, Freidi. It became known afterwards that Joachim had some stupid Western-style duel with a German student. Joachim removed the black powder and was thereby legally obliged to hang himself on the nearest bridge before the end of the year. Obviously, during that accursed year his playing had a devilish sound."

"How did this matter end?" Freidi enquired.

"Joachim's opponent died of tuberculosis that year."

Freidi drew a deep breath of relief. "Thank God."

"Yes, Freidi. As I said, this is no great tragedy. Joachim felt it and accepted the matter as it was. But in your case, Freidi, the matter is different, that's what I want to talk to you about. We have all felt it and discussed it amongst ourselves.

---

7   Ethics of the Fathers 1:14. Hillel said: "If I am not for myself, who is for me? But if I am for my own self [only], what am I? And if not now, when?"

8   Joseph Joachim (1831-1907), Hungarian Jewish violinist, conductor, composer, and teacher. A close collaborator of Johannes Brahms (1833-1897), he is widely regarded as one of the most significant violinists of the nineteenth century.

"And so?"

"The upshot is, dearest Freidi, that this war within yourself—between your two souls—cannot continue. We feel that, when you play the violin, two souls collide."

Freidi's face became pale.

"Please continue," he burst out impatiently. "Please. I also want . . ."

"It seems to me that you yourself must feel this. Tell me, Freidi, are you really not a Jew?" I asked, although I knew that this was not the case.

Freidi stared at me wide-eyed.

"Don't you know that I'm not Jewish?"

"Hmm."

"It's just . . ."

"Just what?"

"Yesterday I spoke to my mother, who told me that her father's mother—in other words my great grandmother—had a youthful affair with some Jew or other. No, I can't lie to you: not with any old Jew, but with her music teacher Mendelssohn.[9] But after that she married Graf Bellini. Her firstborn son with him was Graf Zádor-Bellini, my mother's uncle, first director of the Budapest Opera. But this all happened such a long time ago and, besides, it doesn't have . . . How can I relate to my great grandmother's youthful love affair, or assign any importance to it? It's nonsense!"

"I don't know, Freidi. Maybe yes, maybe no. But blood plays a significant role in life, especially in art, and you know how complicated the question of first love is. For example, if a maiden who marries a black and doesn't bear him sons then marries a white man, in many cases her firstborn son is either black or half black. I'm telling you, Freidi: the fact that your great grandmother's first love was a Jew—and played an instrument!—rolls a heavy stone from my heart. Freidi, you know that I love you as I love myself, maybe more. I ask you to know who you are. I have told you that you have an inner conflict. It's now clear to me that there is a powerful war going on between your two hands. We have felt for a long time that your left hand is at war with your right hand . . ."

---

9   The descendants of Moses Mendelssohn (1729-1786) all converted, so this is probably fictitious. Felix Mendelssohn Bartholdy (1809-1847) did not greatly enjoy teaching and took only a very few private pupils whom he believed had notable qualities.

Freidi's eyes became round and innocent as those of a bright young boy, and two bright, clear, pearly teardrops illuminated each eye. He lowered his head and said in a purified, quiet voice:

"Yes."

"Yes, Freidi, a war. Thank God that we have at least clarified the issue. Your right hand does its job faithfully and the bow is the faithful servant of all the composer's notes. But your left hand demands its due: your due . . ."

"How will this end?"

"How will it end? It's clear to me that the left hand will either conquer, or wreak revenge on you. Freidi, such revenge is always strange and terrible. I don't want to speak of the devil because then he's sure to appear, but I have experienced such things already."

Freidi sat looking at me with damp eyes and an expression of astonishment. He suddenly rose and laughed. He believed and did not believe.

"You are exaggerating," he said confidently. "It's an exaggeration, even though my mother told me something of the sort. As you know, her uncle the director hanged himself on an organ pipe. But even this story is slightly ambiguous. At the end of the day, what am I to do? If I am not guilty, then . . . What must I do?"

"What you must do? I have no idea, Freidi—be a Jew, that is to say, let your heart and blood be governed by the commands of your emissary the left hand. Try your best—you must succeed, Freidi."

Freidi paced back and forth, rubbed his hands together, and said:

"No! No, my friend, that's impossible. Music isn't a question of politics or religion! Music stands above society, nationality, or religion. I am a musician, an artist—no more nor less. I'll show you how I will compel my left hand to listen to the sacred voices of Grieg, Beethoven, Rubinstein, and all the others.[10] Where they are Jews, I will be a Jew, where they are Hottentots, I'll be a Hottentot."[11]

After that day, I didn't see Freidi until frenzied conscription dragged me to the front line.

---

10   Anton Grigoryevich Rubinstein (1829-1894), Russian composer and pianist.

11   Ethics of the Fathers 2:5. "Where there are no men, try to be a man"; Hameiri liked to use African images as a metaphor for wildness and barbarism. Hottentot is a term historically used to refer to the Khoikhoi, the non-Bantu indigenous, nomadic pastoralists of South Africa.

2.

Now, when for more than a year I am losing what's left of my life in these death pits, Freidi has suddenly reappeared beside me. I cannot describe our meeting here in normal terms, just as it is impossible to describe the meeting of two old friends in the slaughterhouse of the front line. The tie with which a joyful life binds two kindred souls differs from one that unites the two in death. It is a kind of lofty, sad synthesis of two souls that no man can understand. Its source lies beyond life and death, and unites the thousand individual parts of our nature into one universal unit. There is no love like one sanctified under the black canopy of nothingness. This kind of love can only be expressed in the midst of the terrible symphony of cannon fire and death groans of thousands of God's creatures who kill without hate any and are killed without "why" and the sorrow of "why."[12]

Freidi's violin comes as a blessed intermezzo in the midst of this mysterious, horror-filled symphony. It revives us with its episodes of joyful song, which cure, soften, and drug the senses. At times when battle ceases for a day or two, when both we and the miserable wretches on the other side of the line who are called "the enemy" faint with exhaustion for a few calm moments, Freidi's music acts as a sort of blessed anesthetic which no wine or woman on earth can provide.

For this reason, naturally Freidi is exempt from all commands of war and rough manual activities. He walks amongst us like a symbol of life which we have suddenly lost. A symbol of the city that has sent us, it's lovers, from its warm bosom, from the rhythmic applause of its beauty that lulls us into a drunken sleep—out into the thunder of war. It has sent us into the din of combat and the heart of darkness, to defend and watch over it and, if necessary, die on the altar of its peace, the defiled and sacred together. At times like these, Freidi's violin sprinkles the scent of the city onto our forlorn souls. Our colonel[13] also finds it wonderful and watches over Freidi like the apple of his eye. He quarters with him behind the lines, eats, drinks, and does the rounds with him. Gradually Freidi's name acquires special significance, even to the lowliest private. In the city one had to look for connoisseurs who understood his art. But here, the simplest farmer sheds secret tears when Freidi plays even the most abstract aria. When Freidi enters the front lines, he fills us with the

---

12   Hameiri uses *madua*, which refers to the past.

13   The biblical term *Sar haelef* (Hebrew) has no modern equivalent.

very essence of his sensitive soul, which overflows with child-like life and the hope of spring and nature's universal secrets.

And this soul is Jewish. How is it recognized as Jewish? What signs signify it? It's impossible to know this clearly. Go out and learn,[14] search and isolate it logically: Why does Ambrosio's sonata weep like a Jewish lamentation under his hands?[15] From the most common farmer-soldier who has only passed by a synagogue once in his life to the colonel who conducted an orchestra and chorus at home, all of us feel the sorrow of a Jewish soul in his playing: caressing, protesting, angry, hopeful, and touchingly atoning for real or imagined insults at the same time.

Freidi becomes a kind of idea to us. That idea is synonymous with another idea, one which all of us feel in our inmost souls, and only the devil who fights, struggles, attacks, and kills the soldier on the line can overshadow this concept, at least for a while. He tries to hide it, but, no matter what, it still demands to burst out into the open.

That idea is peace.

I am not sure how it happens, but when Freidi plays we don't long for physical peace. We feel an inner peace, in which and for which we have been born. It blossoms and prospers in our very blood. We don't hope for it because it has already been achieved and reigns in our hearts and souls. This occurrence has driven our physics professor Dr. Maising out of his mind with joy. On our part, we consider it a miracle. Each time Freidi plays for us for a few minutes, shooting on both sides stops at once—even shots fired during times of rest stop. All along the line wherever his playing penetrates, a sort of tender silence suddenly arises—a calm filled with secrets. A sort of reciprocal command on both sides not to disturb the hearts of those who apparently do not hate each other: quite the contrary.

In the beginning it is considered a miracle, but interpretations soon follow. Professor Dr. Maising tries to explain it by sound waves. According to his theory, the First Cause[16] of all living movement and creative change, even

---

14   The Pesach *hagada* begins the exposition of the Exodus from Egypt with: "Go out and learn what Laban the Aramean sought to do our father Jacob."

15   Alfredo D'Ambrosio (1871-1914), Italian composer and violinist.

16   Argument in natural theology and natural philosophy in which the existence of God is inferred from alleged facts concerning causation, explanation, change, motion, contingency, dependency, or finitude with respect to the universe or some totality of objects. Traditionally known as an argument from universal causation or argument from first cause.

movement of astronomical objects, is reflected by the waves of heavenly symphony. Every universal form is the embodiment of rhythm, beginning with star-shaped snowflakes that differ in proportional exactness and end in the starry skies and Heavens of the Creation, whose qualities and quantities no man can fathom. Dr. Maising's enthusiasm doesn't cool until he shows us the well-known experiment of filtered sand grains on a sheet of glass. When a violin bow is drawn over the tip of the sheet, grains gradually gather in the shape of small crystalline stars which look miraculously like snowflakes—these are the various rhythmic forms that are visible to the naked eye. The Egyptian Bridge in St. Petersburg[17] is another example—no other explanation for what happened has been found. Once, a unit of Tsar Paul I's soldiers[18] crossed over it—the same mad tsar who was so laughably punctilious about parades and ceremony. While they were crossing the bridge in "watch parade"-style, it suddenly split in two and collapsed. All experts decided (and their decision still holds) that the bridge, which weighed 180,000 times more than the soldiers who crossed it, could only have been destroyed by the rhythm which accidentally passed through intersectional waves of the bridge's atoms. "How else can you explain destruction of the walls of Jericho after the sound of the seven shofars of Joshua's priests?" asks Dr. Maising with righteous indignation. "What is that compared to silencing a few tired soldiers? If this is all like water off a duck's back to you," the physics professor asks our senior officers, "why are you so wary as to lead your troops without rhythm, in 'irregular formation,' when you cross bridges?"[19] Dr. Maising goes out of his mind with the joy of finally arguing and convincing us in favor of the sacred truths which he feels to be self-evident and for which he has devoted his academic and personal life.

Others amongst us explain the issue in a disparaging way. According to one, the explanation is simple. There are many Jews on both sides of the line, who influence their comrades with their intelligence: when they hear the "Jewish tune," they immediately silence their guns. There are many such

---

17   The Egyptian bridge in St. Petersburg, originally built in 1825-1826, carries Lermontovsky Prospect over the Fontanka River. It collapsed on 1905 and was rebuilt in 1955, including the original Egyptian-style columns, ornaments, and hieroglyphics.

18   Tsar Paul I was born in 1754 and assassinated in 1801. Hameiri is being sarcastic: the bridge was built twenty-four years after his death.

19   *Halacha mekulkelet*: untranslatable wordplay. Although there are thirty-nine categories of prohibited work on the Sabbath, it is permitted to repair something that is damaged (*mekulkal*). The Hebrew word *halacha* can mean both "walk" and "Jewish ritual law."

explanations. But no matter what, one thing is clear. Freidi's playing has spread a kind of blue protective kerchief of dreams, rest, and love over us, that endangers our discipline and desire for victory. Hearts soften, sinews tremble and weaken, and mouths used to cursing vulgarities and biting start yearning for kisses and embraces.

"Peace! Peace! Universal Peace!" This is the melody that flows from young Freidi's violin.

"If peace does come soon," our colonel smiles, under the influence of Freidi's playing, "I promise that his violin will have brought it, because or in spite of dumb diplomacy."

But in the midst of this peace I feel the presence of another war, a second war of hidden worlds, distant and ancient at the same time. Quite obviously, only a few of us feel the presence of this unseen but potentially powerful war. Freidi is one of them.

This unseen war is fast approaching its end.

I have seen this war coming for quite a while. Freidi's violin playing has become a terror, a monstrosity, a silent anxiety. When I listen to him, I am gripped by an unfounded fear, as if I am waiting for something . . . In recent days I have hidden myself and fled from him and his violin. But fate catches up with us.

Evening has fallen and the setting sun sheds its golden spring glow onto us. The spring weather is enough to drive soldiers in this hell of death and suffering out of their minds. We have been in our dugout for six days now, without any preparation for battle. During this lull in the fighting all we hear above us are shots to fulfill the minimal obligation of war, since complete cessation is forbidden all along the line. But even now it's impossible to show our heads above the dugout. The lines are so close that not only a head, but even a hand, draws enemy fire. An exposed head means certain death. An exposed hand means death before a firing squad, because it's a sign that a man wants to get a "million dollar wound," which would relieve him from front line duty and send him home. A court martial and death by firing squad will surely follow.

Freidi comes up to me and whispers with a smile on his face that he wants to get wounded, just a little. First, to return home for a few weeks and second, as a sign of bravery and the glory that goes with it—a wounded officer: that would be something special! I warn him how dangerous what he is suggesting is: he could be executed by firing squad for this. Freidi laughs and says embarrassedly: "By my life it isn't me, but my evil inclination, that tempts me to do this. I live an excellent life here: the colonel extends every kindness to me. But every time I enter the dugout, it's as if a devil grabs my hand and pushes it upwards."

My blood freezes, but I remain silent. Suddenly the spirit takes me: I rise and hurry to the telephone: I want to tell the colonel about this. I know how he loves Freidi and that he would forgive his ugly stupidity and prevent it from happening. But the line is busy. I regret my original decision: this would be a betrayal of a talented man, guilt by suspicion. He has not done anything yet and will most probably never will.

It happens in the evening. The isolated firing doubles in intensity. Freidi takes up his violin and begins to play in the pleasant but sorrowful evening twilight. I sit on my bench a few yards away in front of my cave and try unsuccessfully to close my ears, so as not to listen. He who hasn't heard the melody of a violin virtuoso rising from the pit of hell when evening falls, he who hasn't listened to music emanating from the soul of a soldier who lives and suffers under the wings of that miraculous angel named death—he will never understand or guess at the secret of the seven voices[20] mixing with the seven colors[21] to yield a mysterious harmony filled with eternal wonder and blessed harvest. They flow from the soldier's soul, living and suffering under the omnipresent wings of the Angel of Death. Freidi's melody resonates in thousands of suffering soldiers' hearts at once. In the beginning I don't know the melodies that he is playing, but later I recognize them. He is playing: "Lieder ohne Worte."[22] The violin begins to swallow up the bullets and artillery shells flying over our heads in rasping lines into air and soul, absorbs and elevates them into a strange but pleasant harmony, accursed and wonderful at the same time. Eventually the melody swallows up the firing completely: gradually the sounds of death become silent under the soft, warm, quiet evening sky which spreads its healing bluish-red canopy of peace over all beneath it.

Suddenly—a voice like that of a decapitated bird cuts through the air: the melodic meter has been severed.

---

20 Psalm 29:3-9.

21 The seven colors of refracted light and therefore of the rainbow.

22 *Songs Without Words*, a series of short, romantic piano pieces by Felix Mendelssohn (see note 9).

The dream is cut off in the middle. Breathless silence, no movement. After a moment, a silent shriek tears at the heart and nerves. It's Freidi's voice. After another moment I hear: "Freidi is wounded!"

"Where is he wounded?"

"In the hand."

I hurry to Freidi, pick him up off the ground, and my heart almost stops beating. The bullet has pierced the tendons of his left arm, between hand and elbow.

The colonel runs around like a madman. He understands at once how shameful this is. His own Freidi has mutilated himself—shame and disgrace! The soldiers look at each other. Terrible! What will happen now? A firing squad?

There is no court martial. The colonel successfully manages to blur the issue and make it go away.

The next day a new rumor does the rounds in the trenches, even more terrifying than the first. The physician finds that the bullet that wounded Freidi was slightly rusted, preventing the wound from healing properly. The wound becomes infected. There is only one way to save him: *amputate the hand at once*. Delay will prove fatal.

The news burns like a suffocating forest fire. Freidi's left hand must be amputated . . . like a useless rag . . . Freidi's hand . . . how can this be?

The war does us a favor by diverting our attention. The same day, the enemy storms our positions and we forget about the whole terrible business.

3.

I don't hear anything about Freidi until I myself am wounded and brought to the regimental hospital in a state of shock. My wound is deep and dangerous, but I have not forgotten about Freidi. I ask the doctor whether he knows where he is and am astonished at his reply:

"Freidi has been in the insane asylum," the doctor replies. "I believe that he died two days ago."

I don't remember what happened after that—the pain from my wound overwhelms me.

A few days later, the nurse tells me the following:

"The whole matter is so strange that it was discussed in the newspapers. Freidi asked the doctor to give him his hand back after it was amputated. The doctor, who knew him from before, did what he asked, as a matter of exception—a hand like that! . . . We all wept. The doctor embalmed the hand as was usual in such cases; he placed it in a glass box overlaid with silver and gave it to him. The box was placed on the small table next to his bed. It was amazing—the young man lay quietly without complaint or despair, like one who has accepted his suffering and sacrifice with love. After that came the news that the Music Academy wanted to put the hand in their museum, but Freidi refused. 'I won't give it to any academy in the world!' Naturally they didn't persist. The unfortunate young man lay in silence: he didn't even become angry at what had happened and allowed the stump to be dressed without complaint. Only once did he start to complain that his head ached. He suddenly asked that the box be removed from his table—he didn't want it, he said with a painful sigh. When we wanted to do as he asked, he changed his mind. No, he wouldn't give his hand to anyone else! One night he jumped up from the bed and began to scream. I hurried to him immediately and found him in a disheveled, confused state. When I asked him what the matter was, he said that he was afraid to reveal the secret to me.

"'What secret?' I asked him with astonished laughter. He started to weep.

"'Nurse,' he said with tears in his eyes, 'dear, beautiful nurse, the hand wants to strangle me—to strangle me.'

"'What do you mean strangle?'

"'Yes, sweet nurse . . . it is strangling me . . . look at my neck . . . the hand is still alive.'

"'You are foolish, Freidi, calm down. A dear, sacred hand like this can't strangle anyone, least of all you. Calm down, you are just tired.'

"'No, dearest nurse. It wants to strangle me, to kill me with its five fingers . . . Each time I fall asleep, it gets out of the box, crawls onto my chest like a spider, grabs my neck, and begins to strangle me. The hand is very strong, dearest nurse.'

"'Dearest Freidi, you are tired and overwrought. Calm down, it's just a foolish dream.'

"He didn't listen to me.

"'Nurse, please don't leave me, don't go out of the room, please stay here . . .'

"'Yes, dear Freidi, I will stay with you. But perhaps, with all this, it would be best to give the hand to the academy?'

"The young man got up from the bed, as if he wanted to save the box and prevent anyone from stealing it by protecting it with his right hand.

"'No, God forbid,' he said in a hoarse but threatening voice. 'It's my hand. No one dare touch it! But it's strangling me,' he added. His hand became limp and fell from the box, and he started to implore me again: 'Dear nurse, don't leave me, don't go!'

"He fell over and started to weep like a madman. In all my years as a nurse in this hospital, I have never heard such weeping. He closed his tear-filled eyes and began to murmur softly, as if to himself:

"'I know . . . I know . . . It will strangle me . . . It won't rest until it strangles me. The Jewish hand will take revenge on me. Dearest nurse, please speak to it, pacify it. It's not my fault. By my life, it's not my fault at all! . . .'

"Not understanding what he was saying I kissed him and he fell asleep. He was as tired as a soldier after heavy fighting.

"Towards morning, Freidi's terrible yelling awakened me. He screamed with all his weakened strength:

"'Save me! Mercy! Save me!' he screamed insanely; his wide eyes fixed on the box. 'That cursed hand is strangling me! Just now it returned to its place! Look at my neck! Can't you see the five fingers? Look how the fingers are bent and twisted like a spider!'

"We looked at the hand in the box and our blood froze. The fingers were indeed bent and twisted. The box was half open. Freidi must have opened it, but the doctors were amazed: How could an embalmed, dried-up hand change its form? Only the old professor nodded saying, as if to himself, like one who reveals a little but conceals a lot:

"'Yes, this is unheard of anatomically, yes, yes, anatomically, anatomically.' The old man spoke with a kind of despairing mockery. 'Anatomy. Are there any friends or relatives here?'

"Two hours later, poor Freidi's mother paid him a visit. I didn't speak to her because to do so was impossible. But the professor started up a quiet, private conversation with her. Afterwards I saw the professor nodding his head wisely as if understanding everything. 'Anatomy . . .'

"That same day, they transferred the boy to an insane asylum. They had to transfer the amputated hand with him because, without it, it was impossible to coerce him or calm him down in his overexcited state. This tender young man had the strength of Hercules.

"A few days later we heard that Freidi had died. It was said that, before he died, he repeated again and again that the hand was strangling him. When they found his body, the box was broken, with the hand standing on his chest, supported by its five fingers. The coroner determined: death by strangulation. On his neck were the blue marks of five fingers."

Satan's Idyll[1]

The square: an infernal cemetery,
cursed calm in the pit,
the celestial provision supplied,
(its belly full of human flesh)
spring wonders are sunlit.

The sun: in all its glory,
has cracked the clouds of splendor;
and flower lusts for flower:
(blood-thirsty love fiend)
breed, kiss me tender.

All around: rotting dead,
decomposing in putrid steam,
while the slaughter-ground is sleeping,
(oh, wretched whore-bred whore)
digesting corpses in its dream.

And atop a congealed, dirty flower
slowly descends a bee—
How peculiar!—It buzzes puzzled,
(oh, perverse life divinity!)
while nursing blood with glee.

---

1   Avigdor Feuerstein, "Idilyat Hasatan," in *Masu'ot: Collections Dedicated to the Questions of The Times, Studies and Literature*, ed. Moshe Glickson (Odessa: Omanut Publishing, 1919), 323.

On the Verge[1]

> "If you dare kiss me when I die; you will die twice" From my grandfather's will.

For Marya Ravlovitz, a victim of truth.

One of the worst in a number of accursed nights of terror.

We have been killing each other for thirty-six consecutive hours, day and night, without stopping. No rest, no food or drink, no sleep.

Even the flashes of rifle and artillery fire don't illuminate the pitchy darkness.

We are going mad walking in this thick blackness. We use bayonets and swords to spear, stab, slash, skewer, punch holes in each other, with savagery, screaming, wild anger, biting, cursing, moaning, groaning, roaring, in clothes soaked with sweat, rain, trudging ankle deep in the thick Galician mud that sucks us down onto our hands and knees, and from which we arise laboriously, only to once again lock horns, struggle, wrestle, hit, and stab in the air, in the foggy darkness, mindlessly, without power or purpose, with fragmented, hoarse moans and our last strength.

Sometimes we skewer each other instead of the enemy, who simply disappear in the darkness one after the other, and our hands move almost on their own . . .

To the point of exhaustion.

Suddenly the order comes—rest.

Such an order requires no explanation. It is obeyed on the spot.

We throw ourselves on the ground and, in a moment, are fast asleep.

"Pály!" I call out to my batman.

"Here I am!" I hear near me in the darkness.

---

1   Avigdor Feuerstein, "Al Hasaf," *Rimon* 1, no. 10 (1922), 32-35.

He gropes towards me, crawling on all fours.

"Please, sir. Come here. You are lying in stinking mud. It's better here."

He grabs me by the hand, leads me a few steps back, and points: "Here. Lie down alongside me."

I drop to the ground and lie in the mud. But where my head rests it is somewhat more comfortable: soft, warmer, more pleasant.

My batman has chosen a good spot.

My eyes close automatically: in a moment I'll be asleep.

But the ground underneath me seems to be moving up and down.

It's nothing, just my heart beating. My nerves are stretched so tightly that I cannot distinguish one thing from another.

My legs stretch out and my hands drop down pleasantly, my heart slows down, and my brain is immersed in sweetest darkness.

Pály is already snoring.

Suddenly there is a slight murmuring and movement around me, like men suddenly getting up and running for their lives.

What does this mean?

I ask but don't ask, and don't move.

What will be will be.

Pály's snoring stops.

Is he running away as well?

Sleep is so sweet, what is this to me? What will be will be.

Suddenly, a foot kicks my head.

"Get up, you bastard!"

It's pitch dark. I don't open my eyes, but still see clearly:

A tall Cossack officer has kicked me. In one hand he holds a long bayonet, in the other a human head, held by the hair.

I am not scared. What can I do? I get up and go with him.

Where are my weapons? If I had my rifle, I could shoot him.

I have neither batman nor weapons. My entire company has upped and run away.

I go with the Cossack to their part of the front.

Why don't I escape?

It's too late. All my men have fled and I am left all alone.

I walk in front of him. A second Russian appears on one side, a third on the other.

I have been taken prisoner.

They speak to each other. I don't understand a word. If they were speaking Russian, I could at least understand a few words, but the language they are speaking is completely different.

I listen and understand: they are speaking Cossack.

Yes, it's the Cossack language.[2]

Is there really a Cossack language? There must be one, because they are speaking it. We approach a large tree.

The tree is surrounded by light.

Where does the light come from?

It comes from between the tree branches.

"Halt!"

I obey.

"To the tree!"

I walk to the tree.

"Turn around!"

I turn around facing the tree.

Two Cossacks grab both my hands, twist them behind my back, and wrap them around the tree trunk. I want to cry out, but they reassure me:

"Don't be afraid, *Pan*.[3] Don't be afraid: it won't hurt."

And truly, I do not fear pain. My hands are twisted behind me around the wide tree trunk, almost to the point of fracturing. Yet I feel no pain.

The Cossack who kicked while I was asleep stands before me, takes his sidearm out, and says:

"Now you will die, *Pan*."

I knew all along that I am going to die, but nevertheless my hair stands on end and my heart beats uncontrollably.

He raises his pistol and says: "Open your mouth so I can shoot you through it."

My eyes bulge out of my head, my mouth twists shut, and my face contorts like that of a child trying to flee from a raging bull in a confined space.

'Open your mouth, *Pan*!"

I prevent myself from bursting out in an attack of weeping.

"Don't, *Pan*," I stammer weepingly, "please don't."

---

2   Hameiri is probably referring to Balachka, the dialect of Ukrainian spoken by the Cossacks of the North Caucasus, especially around the Kuban River.

3   Sir.

I am instantly ashamed of my fear and cowardice. He brings his pistol up to my face and smiles:

"Don't, *Pan*, please. Why are you doing this? You are deluding yourself. Please don't.

Why? I'm not the enemy. I love you. I . . ."

"Open your mouth!"

I open my mouth.

Why am I so stubborn? Why don't I stand up straight and die like a man? It would make no difference anyway.

He smiles:

"Now you are going to die. In your mouth. Do you wish to die?"

"No, dear *Pan*. No. To live. I . . ."

"Silence! Open up, so that I can put a bullet through your lying mouth!"

He thrusts the pistol into my mouth.

Two hot tears splash onto my cheeks. My body shakes violently. I close my eyes and wait.

The cold steel touches my teeth, tongue, and palate.

I wait, drenched with sweat.

He removes the pistol from my mouth and smiles.

"No, not in your mouth. In your neck."

I open my eyes in relief and smile. He is playing with me.

He presses the hard steel onto my neck.

I close my eyes shudderingly and wait.

"No," he says, "straight into your cursed heart."

I open my eyes.

He opens my tunic and points the pistol at my heart.

"Here, here, into your sick heart."

My heart stops beating and I feel a choking sensation.

"Please, *Pan*. You're a good man. An upright man of intelligence. Please don't."

'Yes, I am a good man. Straight into your black heart."

He presses the pistol onto my chest and smiles.

But now I see that it's my brother, not a Russian officer. Yes—my brother. My brother, who is serving in the German army.

"Istvan! Is that you?" I let the words slip out joyfully and calmly. "Istvan, is that you? Tell them to let me go. What do they want? They are hurting me."

He answers calmly:

"I've been dead for a month already and you didn't even mourn my passing. You didn't shed a single tear. Our mother also died four months ago, yet you laugh. Do you want to die as well?"

He bends over and kisses me.

He isn't my brother. My feverish brain has conjured up an imaginary image. He really is a Russian murderer who is abusing me. Terrible. It's my fate to die, to leave my mother and dear brother.[4]

He removes the pistol from my heart and aims it at my belly.

"Yes, a belly shot. Do you know?—a belly wound causes terrible agony. Food leaks out of the intestines."[5] I know that. I can hear in my mind the screams of someone dying from a belly wound from miles away. His cries rise up to heaven and cleave the blue-black clouds in two.

My intestines convulse and I weep soundlessly:

"Please, *Pan*, I: implore you out of the goodness of your heart. I promise you. You are a good man. You are my brother Istvan . . ."

"Yes, a good man. Turn your head aside and expose your temple. I'll shoot you in the temple."

I turn my head to the side, exposing my temple.

What's happening? Instead of Russians, a woman's hands are grasping me.

It's Margit. All my love and warmth well up in my boiling blood.

"Margit, my little golden bird, dearest orphan, sweet betrothed, all my hope and joy—he wants to kill me!"

She doesn't turn to me or listen to what I am saying.

"Margit, is it you or not? Margit Verdesi . . ."

She lets go of my hand, evades me, and lies down in the mud.

I want to approach her and pick her up but cannot move. My hands are twisted behind me, wrapped around the tree.

Suddenly my mind clarifies: it's just a dream. Thank God. My blood flows like a warm, healthy spring. How stupid of me: of course, it's a dream. How could Margit have arrived here? At the front line?

Yes, I see everything in a dream. I am dreaming and know that I am dreaming. I see her lying on the muddy ground, pale and yellow, dead—it's a dream.

---

4   Hameiri's mother died when he was a young boy.

5   In the pre-antibiotic era, wounds that perforated the intestines were uniformly fatal due to peritonitis.

But I still feel the cold gun metal pressing against my temple.

No, it isn't a dream. He is going to kill me by a shot through the temple. I wait. In a moment the bullet will penetrate my brain and I will die.

"Please, *Pan*. I implore you. Kill me now. Shoot me and kill me now. I wish to die. Just don't torture me."

He removes the pistol from my temple and says:

"No, I won't kill you with a pistol, not with a bullet. I'll kill you with my bayonet. I'll run you through, like you killed my friend Artur. I'll thrust my bayonet through your open mouth."

He turns to one of the soldiers standing in a line behind him, saying:

"Give me your bayonet."

The soldier gives him his rusty bayonet. He points it at my mouth and starts to thrust it in very slowly and deliberately. I don't yet feel any pain, but my blood boils and sizzles. My heart weakens and begins to die. I feel the sharp tip of the bayonet in my palate. My mind begins to darken. I close my eyes—

"Oy . . ."

He pulls the bayonet out, looks at me with eyes wide with disgust, fixes his two red pupils on me, and screams quietly but with terrible fury:

"You buried my brave father in a filthy latrine! My father!"

I open my eyes. It isn't the officer who is screaming at me, but a pale thirteen-year-old boy. He adds angrily and tearfully:

"It was my sainted father who you buried in the filthy latrine! I know where: it was in the village of Lazarovka near the von Wilitzki Palace.

"Quiet! I'll puncture you like a sieve!"

He begins to wave the bayonet tip in front of my face, eyes, brain, belly, and throat with rapid, thrusting movements. I hold my breath and feel that I am choking; my whole body trembles. The bayonet hovers with terrible rapidity over my tied-up body. In a moment it will penetrate me. My spirit fades . . .

"*Pan*, my friend: my father, Margit my beloved, Istvan, my mother— please don't torture me. Kill me right now, I implore you: bless me by thrusting the bayonet into me. Oy—Oy—"

He thrusts the bayonet through my mouth and palate, deep into my brain. Oy, I feel pain. My heart stops beating. I feel a warm, pleasant but terrible bubbling throughout my body. I hold my breath. Death—gruesome death. My blood boils with terror—I am dead. The end. All is lost, everything . . .

He removes the bayonet from my mouth and says:

"That's it. He's dead. Let's go. Let the loathsome carcass rot here."

I fall down dead on the ground. I am dead. Good.—So what? My throat hurts a little—that's all. I am released from of all fear and sorrow, all terror, suffering, and war, from dark nights, hunger, and mud. I am saved from death itself! Is that all? No more? And now . . ?

I draw a relieved breath: restful, appeasing, peaceful and blessed.

Ah hah!

I feel an inner happiness of infinite light and joy beyond measure.

"Released from everything, free, free forever to do as I please."

Margit rises from the ground and comes up to me.

She closes my weak eyes and kisses me.

I want to rise and pour my infinite love into her but restrain myself. It could yet be a dream. May it continue. So pleasant it is!

Then, she removes my clothes.

Then, my skin, polluted by blood and wounds.

After that, she removes my tired flesh and pain-saturated bones, and says:

"My naïve sweet man. So naïve. Were you startled? You have suffered greatly. You imagine that this is terrible. I was also afraid in the beginning, my naïve dear. But you are free now."

She caresses me, saying:

"They're still standing here, but you have nothing to fear. They don't control you anymore. Rise upwards with me."

I embrace her and float to the top of the tree.

I am light as a feather, sans clothes, flesh, and body. Sans brain, bones, aching heart. I rise upward, ever upward.

But the officer and his men sense it. They pursue me and climb the tree:

"He's alive!" they yell. "He's alive! The bastard! He escaped!"

Some of them climb onto the tree, others aim their weapons at me. Dozens of rifles open up on me. I hold my breath. I am seized with horror. If they kill me now—everything is finished!

"Margit!" I moan, "Margit! Margit!"

Suddenly—rifle fire—dead silence.

The rifle fire hasn't made a sound. Nothing has touched me.

The bullets have entered my body, but haven't touched me.

I am shocked to the marrow of my bones. I am gripped by a light, stuporous ferment, sprout wings, and fly! I fly high in the air! I don't think of what will happen afterwards. Like a child sheltering in the arms of his mother after a terrible event, I laugh loudly and my whole body is suffused with happiness.

"Ha-ha-ha!"

How absurd! Is this death? How absurd!

I awake.

It's already morning: damp, dreary, disgusting.

I try to turn on my side and suddenly hear:

"Sir, an order has just come in!"

I open my eyes and see Pály before me and a soldier handing me an order from headquarters.

I take it and read:

"This evening, General Artur Guthagen and his batman both disappeared. We have found out that hate drove the batman to murder the general in a most cruel way. His body must be found immediately. Whoever finds it will be highly decorated. The name of the murderer is Andras Bandari. He has a scar on his forehead. The commander in chief."

I have hardly finished reading the order when Pály informs me:

"Sir, I know where His Excellency's body is. I will go and bring it back! Please give me two men."

I am tired. I give him the men and say sluggishly:

"Go and hand the order to the sergeant."

I want to go back to sleep.

Suddenly I see a dead body on the spot I had used as a pillow during the night.

Hell and damnation!

Some papers are sticking out of his pockets. Amongst them I find a letter:

"Andras my darling, beloved of my heart and soul:

"This will be my last letter. I cannot go on anymore. I am tired and wretched, a miserable orphan. During the past few days I moved in with your dear mother. She was my last refuge. She received me like her own child and I was happy with her. Suddenly she died. At about the same time she was being buried, news came from the German army that your brother Istvan has fallen, and yesterday I dreamed that you too had died. Why should I remain alive? Farewell. If you perchance remain alive, come to my grave and die there.

"Your miserable beloved, Margit Verdesi."

I rub my eyes. What is going on?

Istvan . . . Margit . . . Verdesi . . . Andras . . .

I have never known these names before. But I know them . . . I know . . . How?

I examine the address on the letter.

"To Andras Bandari, the soldier who serves as batman for the Herr General Guthagen, etc."

With great restraint, I retain my self-control and try to understand what is going on.

The dead man whose body I used as a pillow during the night is Andras Bandari.

He is General Guthagen's batman, under sentence of death for his general's murder and being looked for everywhere.

He is the murderer whom everyone is seeking.

Margit Verdesi is his beloved. Yes, Margit . . .

It is she who told him that his brother Istvan was killed in the German army.

I know all of this . . .

I am still thinking and wondering about it all when Pály returns with his two men, bringing back the body of the dead general. It is caked with human excreta in the most horrible way.

"Where did you find the Herr General?

"I found him only a few yards from here, in the Lazarovka village latrine, in the von Wilitzki Palace yard."

I think aloud about his words again:

Lazarovka village . . . von Wilitzki Palace . . . latrine . . .

Pály adds without asking:

"I heard this information from you yourself, sir."

"From me?"

"Yes, from you. You revealed everything in your dream. You cried out in your sleep. I woke up and heard you speaking."

Now I understand everything.

I look at the corpse that I used as a pillow and see a long scar on its forehead.

I feel its chest: the body is still warm.

Was this man really dead while I was lying on him?

His mouth is filled with clotted blood: *he has been stabbed through the mouth.*

Pály adds:

"Now, sir, if I could only succeed in finding the murderer!"

I get up from the ground and show the body to him:

"Ecce homo!"

Kill the Lights[1]

You have extinguished the flame,
shy away from the looking glass.
And if you kill a man—
in his pupil do not glance.

Look not in his eyes,
you shall witness dread, horrors,
and woe unto your heart,
woe unto your coming hours.

You shall witness horrors—
and all the still stiff's glee,
all its burning laughter,
shall resist with cursed plea.

And his world which fades
like pus shall diffuse your blood
and you shall shocked be,
freeze, with madness in slow flood.

So long as you possess your soul,
it shall not absolve nor subside nor shrink,
for you have killed a man—
In your heart thy sword sink.

---

1   Avigdor Feuerstein, "Kill the Lights," in *Masu'ot: Collections Dedicated to the Questions of the Times, Studies and Literature,* ed. Moshe Glickson (Odessa: Omanut Publishing, 1919), 322.

The Spider[1]

1.

Before we had a chance to rest our weary limbs from four consecutive days of fighting, while we were trying to grab some well-deserved beauty sleep, the urgent command came:

"One officer of the scouting corps must take six men with him, attack a machine gun post on the far side of the Dniester River[2] bridge, and bring the gun back, dead or alive!"

The axe fell on eight of us. We were all bone weary, broken, drunk with tiredness, but blessed with good luck at having been saved yesterday from the jaws of death. We lay in one room in a front line dugout, sleeping with varying degrees of restlessness. At least after the terrible fighting we would finally be able to relax for a day or two.

But suddenly the order came.

As it happened, I received the order and called it out loudly. My sense of duty made me the "agent."[3] I really wanted to be the agent, but as soon as I rose from my bed one of my comrades, Captain Walter Amudi, resolutely pushed me back:

"Where in the hell are you going? Lie down in peace, I'll go."

He got up and dressed (not that anyone really got undressed before going to sleep), mumbling as if to himself:

"I'll show that cowardly pig what courage means. If after this he dares to impugn my honor—I'll take him with me to hell. My soul will die with . . ."

Walter Amudi was a Jew—more of a Jew than all of us. He was a very strange young man of about twenty-two, who didn't know the first thing about

---

1   Avigdor Feuerstein, *Ha'Akavish, Doar Hayom* 13, no. 8 (1922), 4.

2   The westernmost of the three great rivers flowing through Ukraine to the Black Sea.

3   Sanhedrin 82a: "Let the one who reads the letter be the agent [*parvanka*] to fulfill its contents."

being a Jew. Before the war, his Judaism was limited to only one thing. Every year, on the anniversary of his mother's death, he went to the cemetery, gave the cemetery warden a gold coin, and planted flowers on his mother's grave. When he was conscripted for war, he went back to the cemetery warden, gave him another gold coin, and said:

"Listen, Jew, this time you must plant an etrog tree[4] on my mother's grave. Do you understand?"

The warden looked at him with bulging eyes: "An etrog?"

Walter Amudi understood his astonishment and explained:

"Why are you surprised about an etrog? I saw such a flowering tree once . . . It's a Jewish fruit and I want it growing on my mother's grave. Is it too expensive?"

He gave him another gold coin and left.

Walter Amudi was a typical Jew.

But a kind of devil intruded into his life during the war, at the front. Walter Amudi was the only Jewish officer who was consumed body and soul[5] by every word or movement aimed at his Judaism. This led to so many acts of bravery that there was no more room on his chest for the medals that he received one after another. All to prove that a Jew falls behind no man in bravery.

And so it was that Walter Amudi joined our scouting company, chest encrusted with bravery medals. As if to anger him, our company was under command of Thaddeus Galzagavi, whose entire raison d'être in this war consisted of insulting and humiliating Jews. Thaddeus Galzagavi was an "officer since birth," and never did an officer have less reason to talk about cowardice in others than he himself did. For this very reason, his baleful glare fixed on Walter Amudi, whose gold and silver medals irritated him immensely. Walter Amudi suffered—he suffered in silence and did what he did. Bravery upon bravery, endangerment upon endangerment. Obviously, he didn't receive a single decoration for valor from Tadeusz Galzagavi. Quite the contrary, he always found fault with him—errors, even cowardice.

For this reason, Walter Amudi volunteered for a job that anyone else would have avoided at all costs. Because with six men it was quite impossible to attack a machine gun post on the other side of the bridge, in which each

---

4   An etrog (citron) is one of the "four species" used on Sukkoth (Festival of Tabernacles).

5   Isaiah 10:18.

man was in such a secure position that it was impossible to approach even with an entire encampment of men.

Walter Amudi placed his six men in line, saying:

"Listen, lads, which of you can swim well?"

All answered, "Yes."

"Good," he said. "Put your rifles down, each of you take a bomb, and tie it on your head. Understand?"

They did so.

The Dniester River bridge belonged to us. We built it and now waited tensely for the enemy to blow it up at any minute. Because we were in "attack mode," we needed the bridge. The enemy stood at its far end, trying with all its might not to abandon their position. We waited tensely and nervously, hoping that our only way towards them would not be cut. It had cost us a great deal of labor to connect both sides of the river.

Walter Amudi left his men and went up to our artillery position.

After a few moments, a deafening explosion erupted. The bridge was torn to pieces and we stood there pale, dejected, almost weeping with disappointment.

At the same time, Walter Amudi returned and said:

"Good! Now let's go." He turned to us: "Why are you all standing there like blocks of cheese? It was I, I myself, who blew the bridge."

"Have you gone mad?"

"No, but an order is an order. I want to capture the machine gun and bring it back here. A few moments ago, I still doubted whether my plot would succeed. But now there is no escape—I am compelled to bring it here. If *he* doesn't take pity on seven of his men and sends them to certain death as scapegoats, let us at least sacrifice the bridge on the altar of their lives. This bridge, my friends, has no mother, no father, no beloved who mourns at home. But we do. Let's go—I'll show that . . !"

They departed.

Meanwhile, dusk fell.

We stood there transfixed, escorting him with our desperate gaze.

After that, we fell asleep.

2.

After a little more than an hour, a powerful cry for help was heard, which woke us up. All of us jumped up and hurried in the direction of the Dniester.

A strange vision, hair-raising and amusing at the same time, rose up before us in the pitch darkness, by the light of the dim moon. Seven men floated in the flowing river, in the direction of our shore. Each one held an object tied behind them in one of their hands.

It was the enemy's machine gun.

Behind them, we saw a second object,

When they crawled out of the water, we saw that it was the body of a man.

Walter Amudi came up to us dragging the dead body behind him. He threw it at our feet, saying:

"Here, my friends, is a gift for that . . ."

He didn't finish what he had to say. Perhaps because of restrained anger, or fear of discipline by "that" commandant. I don't know.

We all shook his hand warmly and with respectful incredulity. He evaded us and went to the telephone.

"Herr Kommandant," he said through the receiver, "your order has been carried out. I also have a gift for you. I have brought you an honored guest, your good friend the machine gun officer. A Russian pig who loves Jews like you do."

Apparently the commandant didn't understand Walter Amudi's venomous hint through the telephone. In a weak tone he told him to go to sleep: he would come to him himself in a few hours' time.

He arrived as promised.

We were all asleep and woke up tired, body and soul aching. Walter Amudi slept on, completely exhausted. The commandant didn't have the strength to wake him up properly, so he spoke to us in a whisper about what had happened. "This really is an important act . . . but . . . the bridge . . . that is a terrible thing. To blow up the bridge . . ."

We were astonished and full of inner disdain at what he had said and tried to calm him down. We tried to convince him that an act of such bravery was worth great sacrifice. We promised him that within the next two days, after the other river bank had been cleared of danger, we would all rebuild the bridge. But it was of no use and the commandant shook his head in complaint and derision.

Suddenly, Walter Amudi became pale and awoke in panic. He lashed out violently with his arms and legs and cursed violently. He leapt from the bed in terrible fear, face white as a sheet and eyes bulging out of their sockets. He looked frozenly at the bed, consumed with fear. We all went up to him but he pointed to the sheet: "Hell and damnation—there it is!—Miserable vermin—here!—*Brrr*"

He recoiled from the bed and clung to the wall, shuddering.

We looked at the sheet. A large black spider sat there, watching us.

When the commandant saw this, he fixed his eyes penetratingly on Walter Amudi, then went up to him and said with terrible contempt:

"The 'Herr Offizier' is afraid of a spider. That's wonderful, really wonderful! A chest full of medals—and you're scared of a spider. That's fine! Shame and disgrace! The Herr Offizier is not entitled to decorations for what he has done! Better that they all be removed from his chest!"

We all stood like blocks of marble. Walter Amudi stood for a moment, eyes bulging like a calf. His entire body trembled and he was shocked to his depths of his soul. He went up to the commandant, so close that their faces nearly touched, and began to scream, almost into his mouth:

"Herr Kommandant! My war decorations? My war decorations?! War decorations cannot be removed![6] By my life and soul, I earned each one of mine!"

He balled his fist as if wanting to hit him, but thought better of it. He suddenly came up to the bed, took the spider, brought it up to the commandant's mouth, and screamed: "Take this, Herr Kommandant! Take this! If you are so brave—take this!"

He thrust the spider into the commandant's mouth.

The commandant's whole body trembled and he recoiled backwards, stammering a few words. Walter Amudi paced to and fro as if looking for something and uttered a terrible scream:

"Friends! Where is my revolver? This bastard has insulted my life! This coward, who has polluted my soul! Where is the revolver? He shall die like a dog!"

He found the revolver and shot the commandant with all six bullets one after the other. He dragged the dead body outside, threw it next to the body of the dead Russian officer, and snorted:

"There you are! There is your friend: a hero like yourself!"

He kicked both furiously and burst out into a fit of wild, terrible, mad laughter.

---

6   After Beitzah 30a.

On Guard[1]

Who walks there?
Stop and state!
(No need for arms,
I am a brother, a mate).

All who pass here
shall die by the sword!
What say you? Speak!
(Our Lord).

Where have you come from?
Approach, at ease.
(I have brought thee a gift,
eternal peace).

Who are you? What is your name?
Front and center!
(I am the Angel of Death).
By all means, enter.

---

1   Avigdor Hameiri, "*Al Hamishmar*," *Ta'am Mita, Ha'olam* (Berlin) 7, no. 2 (1923), 8.

A Blessed Fall Dawn[1]

*(To my great, revered brother Rabbi Zanvil Yarden,
with recognition and confidence)*

We stand on watch, shivering with cold, with tired eyes and weary bones, eyes fixed on the enemy front line. We stand in our trenches, pouring out our hearts melted with stifled song into the fall morning gradually covering the fields and meadows, mountains, and withered aftergrowth with a golden glow. The fields have remained untended for the past two years.

A blessed fall dawn.

The yellowish grass, embracing the trampled harvest that no one has gathered, shines with thousands of slivers of wintry dew, binding each stalk together into strings of pearly drops. These white fall threads, called "ox saliva" by simple farmers, cover the quiet, wide expanse of fields with an endless net from horizon to blue horizon. Dewdrops without number glisten on these white threads without anyone trampling on or disturbing them.

They remain undisturbed, because neither man nor beast can pass over and remain alive. They are surrounded by thousands of gaping rifle barrels.

All our wretched wishes and desires radiate into this magical, wondrous net, gilded by the rising sun.

Someone says:

"Happy is he who will be the first to wash his feet in this dew without danger of being killed, with a song of peace on his lips."

We all stand entranced, staring into the distance.

The battalion commander awakens us from our reverie.

"Choose a brave young lad for the day watch" he says to me, "someone who has little respect for death. I've just found out that the enemy is preparing to surprise us today with a little 'game'"

---

1   Avigdor Feuerstein, "Beshahar Stav Mevorach," *Doar Hayom* 12, no. 1 (1922), 5.

This "game" isn't pleasant: it means an incessant rain of unaimed artillery and rifle fire, firing merely for the sake of firing, to scare us and create a disturbance. A sign of life that the enemy neither slumbers nor sleeps.[2]

"Why today?" I ask.

"Stupid question. Today is some sort of Slav holiday, Lord knows them all."

Hardly has he finished speaking when Uncle Osterreicher,[3] who has woken from a few fleeting hours of sleep and been standing on the side, comes up to us and says:

"Sir, please put me on guard duty today!"

Uncle Osterreicher is far from being a "young lad." He is about forty and has several grandchildren at home.

"Has some sort of devil gotten into you, Uncle Osterreicher?"

"No, sir. It's just what I want, sir."

"That's no explanation. Why today? Don't you know that they are going to play their 'game' today?"

"I know, sir, I've heard. But their 'game' doesn't bother me," Uncle Osterreicher emphasizes mockingly. "If Hashem[4] doesn't wish it, who cares what they want?"

He makes a gesture of utter derision.

We're already used to Uncle Osterreicher's disparagement of the enemy and confidence in his God. But now, we are very curious.

"Despite everything? What on earth do you want there?"

"What I want, Sir? I certainly don't want to die. For a religious Jew like myself, it's expressly forbidden to die a gruesome death before his time. After all, my grandchildren are waiting for me . . ."

"I won't allow it, Uncle Osterreicher. You're right: your small grandchildren are waiting for you. But today, today . . . today's 'game' doesn't take your grandchildren into consideration. Tell me why you insist on this and I'll agree."

Uncle Osterreicher wrinkles his already lined face and says decisively:

---

2   Psalms 121:4.

3   One of Hameiri's comrades during the first two years of the war. A middle-aged Orthodox Jew, he is taken captive by the Russians during a prisoner exchange, but dies of disease on the way to the prisoner of war camp (Avigdor Hameiri, *The Great Madness*, trans. Peter C. Appelbaum [Middletown, RI: Stone Tower Press and Boston, MA: Black Widow Press, 2021]).

4   Name used by Jews for God in lay parlance (The Name).

"Sir, I want to sanctify Hashem's Name!"

"By dying?"

"No, sir. A good Jew doesn't sanctify Hashem's name by dying if it's possible to sanctify it by living!"

I don't agree and want to call upon someone else whose turn it is to stand guard, but the battalion commandant, who has been listening without saying a word, says to me with a smile on his face:

"Let him go. I want to see, for once in my life, how a Jew sanctifies God's name in his life while a thousand deaths await him."

Uncle Osterreicher stands ramrod straight as a sign of thanks and walks to his guard position.

He gets out of the dugout and crawls on all fours to the barbed wire fence on the wet grass.

Suddenly I see some sort of rucksack under his arm.

At first, I think that it's a small bag of sand to serve, as is usually the case, as a shield against bullets, but it doesn't look like that at all. I call out after him:

"What sort of can of worms do you carry under your arm?"

"It's a protective bag," he whispers back at me.

"Nonsense."

"Please believe me, sir, when I say that it really is a protective bag." Uncle Osterreicher turns his unkempt bearded face to me. "There is no protective bag like it in the whole wide world!"

What can I say? We believe him. Uncle Osterreicher is no liar. Sometimes he speaks in foolish riddles, but he would never lie.

Uncle Osterreicher crawls forward until he reaches the barbed wire fence on our side of the line.

There he sits on the wet grass, puts his rifle down, lays the barrel against the barbed wire to keep it dry, and remains there for a few moments facing the enemy front.

We don't even get a chance to look at him properly and promptly enter our dugout when shots ring out.

First a few one by one, then more frequently, from dozens of rifles and mortars, whistling, shaking, exploding, and playing their hellish tunes over our heads.

We escape into our protecting dugout. The bombardment becomes a whistling hail of fire from the mouths of dozens of satanic creatures.

"Poor Uncle Osterreicher," I say to my commandant, "he won't sanctify Hashem's name by living, but by dying."

He looks at me and says:

"I think that you're wrong. You have no idea how much faith I place in Orthodox Jews like him. Laugh at me if you will, but if I had my chance, I would fill my battalion with such Jews. They have something that protects them more than thousands of cannons. Satan or God knows what it is. But as for me, I cannot get away from the perhaps ridiculous belief that now, with the old Jew Jawetz as my batman, I have nothing to fear. You laugh? Nu, good . . . we'll see what happens . . . the enemy will perform its duty today without its 'maftir.'[5] You'll see.

The "maftir" is a shell from the enemy's largest cannon, with which it concludes the "game." It is always aimed at the guards on watch. Without this shell, there is no "game."

The commandant sips some wine, takes his binoculars, and carefully exits the "window" in his dugout, to see what Uncle Osterreicher is doing.

Strange. Our commandant is not a particularly brave man, but he is endangering his life when he doesn't need to. He must really believe in Uncle Osterreicher.

After a minute or so, he calls out to me:

"Quickly, quickly, come over here!"

The firing whistles around us in all its fury, but I still go out, on my commandant's orders.

I stand leaning over the commandant and see something strange. Uncle Osterreicher half rises, sits on his knees and signals to the enemy: he actually summons them.

The shells clatter above his head, but he still calls out to the enemy.

"Perhaps he wants to defect? That would be a very ugly business!"

"Nonsense!" The commandant rebukes me. "Uncle Osterreicher defect? Nonsense! Wait!"

Uncle Osterreicher continues to signal with his two hands and call out to the enemy, who answer with a hail of bullets.

"They don't know Uncle Osterreicher," I say mockingly. "They don't believe him at all."

---

5   Additional reading from the prophets after the Torah reading on Sabbaths and festivals, concluding the Torah service.

"Wait," the commandant rebukes me again.

When Uncle Osterreicher sees that all his movements are in vain, he makes a sign of despair and sits on his knees for a moment. After that, with conviction, he opens his bag and takes something out of it: from this distance it's impossible to see what it is. He puts it on his head under his hat.[6]

The commandant turns to me and says:

"You are a good Jew. Tell me—what is he doing? Do you know what he is doing? He is doing what my old batman does all the time: he is putting on pilin."

"What?"

"Pilin! You're a Jew and don't know that is?"

"Oh yes, tefillin!—that's what it is."

"Shhh—wait!"

Uncle Osterreicher adjusts the tefillin on his head, takes something else from his bag, and puts it on. It's a white tallit.

The commandant is alarmed.

"What is he doing? He's provided a perfect target for the enemy!"

"So what?" I answer mockingly. "It was you who said, honored sir, that you have faith in him."

"You're right. We'll see."

In the meanwhile, we don't even notice that the firing has suddenly stopped and that we are standing up straight, looking around without any fear.

"Nu?" the commandant says victoriously. "Who is right?"

"It's just a coincidence."

"What do you mean coincidence? Where is the 'maftir?' What coincidence?—with you Jews everything is coincidence."

"It's obviously a coincidence. Or more correctly, for some reason they are, for the moment, listening to what he has been doing and saying."

"That may be so. But no matter what, there is no 'maftir' and no death. Let's see what happens next." We observe the developing scene.

Uncle Osterreicher gets up wrapped in tallit and tefillin and indicates further to the Russians.

Through our binoculars, we see the head of a man appearing out of the enemy trench and a hand pointing at Uncle Osterreicher. Uncle Osterreicher

---

6   Strangely, Hameiri doesn't mention Uncle Osterreicher wrapping tefillin on his left arm as well.

answers him. Suddenly another head appears, then another, then an entire man appears from the trench and crawls towards Uncle Osterreicher, followed by more men, one after the other.

Someone stands behind us and says:

"I'll go hunting for them a bit." He aims his rifle at the men.

"To hell with you!" the commandant reprimands him. "Go hunt your grandmother, you idiot!"

The crawlers draw nearer and near Uncle Osterreicher, one after the other.

"He's a traitor!" I say angrily. "He deserves to be executed!"

"Let's see," the commandant says. "Not at the moment. Let's see."

After a few minutes, a small gang of men stands around Uncle Osterreicher, on the other side of the barbed wire. They are swaying back and forth and praying . . .

The sound of prayerful singing becomes louder and the swaying increases.

"What cheek!" the commandant says with an amazed smile. "What unexampled hutzpah!"

He looks at the little gang, limbs swaying together.

They pray without interruption. Behind them the white blinding sun rises and the ten human figures bathe in its abundant light with a magical glow. The ten men are swaying, with expressive movements, standing in death's courtyard with complete, even joyful, confidence. Their singing shakes the still air.

A sudden silence—one voice is heard, clearly intoning the following words, to which we bear witness:

"Yitgadal veyitkadash shmei rabbah."[7]

It's Uncle Osterreicher's voice.

Immediately after that, Uncle Osterreicher takes a small container and a small cup out of his bag, fills the cup and divides it up amongst the ten men. He pours it out and divides it up, pours it out and divides it up . . .

"Lehaim! Lehaim!"[8]

The commandant nearly jumps out of his skin:

"What rascality! "he says, half smiling, half angry—"such Jewish hutzpah! I'll hang him by the strap of his p . . . pil . . . tefillin!"

---

7   Opening words of the mourner's kaddish: "May His great name be exalted and sanctified." (Aramaic).

8   To life.

"That is a long shot, sir," I say. "There will be another 'incident' and he won't die," I say with a hint of mockery.

The little gang acts as if nothing has happened. They drink and prepare to go. Each one stretches his hand out to Uncle Osterreicher.—To our astonishment, he refuses to shake them: "No, please excuse me, but no!"

He doesn't give them his hand. We don't hear what he has said to them, but he refuses to shake their hands.

We look at each other.

The little gang crawls back to their trenches on all fours.

Uncle Osterreicher takes off his tallit and tefillin, puts them back into his bag, and sits on the ground.

He organizes himself, aims his rifle at the enemy, fires three shots at them, and assumes his position at the guard post.

When he returns for duty, he stands "trial" before the commandant. The commandant glares at him, laughing restrainedly.

"Do you know what you are tried for?"

"I know, sir."

"Well?"

"I couldn't do otherwise, sir, I just couldn't."

"Why couldn't you?"

"Today is the anniversary of my wife's death, sir and there is no one to say kaddish for her but me . . . Kaddish is a great thing, sir; it is a sanctification of God's name."[9]

"I'm going to hang you!"

"That would sanctify God's name even more, sir. To sanctify God's name when death awaits is the most genuine form of sanctification. And there was no danger there at all, sir. A man wrapped in tallit and tefillin is protected from the realm of death."[10]

"We'll see! But first tell me why you didn't shake their hands."

Uncle Osterreicher reacts as though a snake has bitten him.

---

9   *Yahrzeit*, anniversary of a loved one's death. Kaddish cannot be recited without a *minyan* (quorum of ten adult Jewish men). Uncle Osterreicher knows that he can easily get a *minyan* amongst Russian, but not his own, troops. The three letter root of *kaddish* and *kedusha* (sanctification) or *kadosh* (holy) is identical.

10   The ultra-Orthodox believe that constant study of Torah and Talmud offers metaphysical protection against disease.

"Me, sir? *I* should offer my hand to the *enemy*?"

The commandant looks backwards so as not to burst out laughing and goes into his room. Hs returns, the remains of a smile on his face, and yells:

"Dismiss and go to hell, you jackass, you old idiot!"

Uncle Osterreicher bolts out instantly and outside he turns to me and says:

"I told you, sir. This is a *protective bag*. It has saved me now from a death sentence."

"What bag? What bag are you talking about?"

Uncle Osterreicher smiles and chuckles confidently. He raises his hat and shows me the tefillin on his head.

"What is this, sir?"

Question and Answer[1]

Tell me, grandfather:
Why is there anguish in this miserable world:
Toil with no pay and hunger and death?
Because, grandson, because there is wealth,
(wealth and death—death and wealth.)

Tell me, grandfather:
Who is to blame for the many
wars and affliction and life which is ruined?
We are to blame, blame the affluent.
(affluent ruined—ruined affluent.)

Tell me, grandfather:
What shall bestow the miserable world
redemption and change and peace and revival?
—Upheaval, oh grandson, upheaval, upheaval.
(Revival, upheaval—upheaval, revival.)

---

1   Avigdor Hameiri, "She'eila Uteshuva," *Ha'Doar* 37 (1924), 7.

Hanale[1]

It's half an hour before midnight.

I stand on guard with two of my men—the "eyes and ears of the" unit.

Standing guard at night, every nerve in the brain becomes an attentive ear. Darkness covers our faces like a layer of black ice. It's impossible to see my own hands, let alone the man standing next to me. But, as if to compensate, pitch darkness sensitizes the ear to every tiny movement, no matter how fine and soft. Darkness blinds the eyes but sharpens the ear and transmits the voice excellently.

After a few seconds, a voice grates on our ears. A kind of hidden, silent weeping trying to restrain itself. The weeping voice is only a few feet away from us. The two enemy lines are very near, separated by only about 250 paces. Almost in the middle on the right-hand side lies the sprawling Jewish cemetery, where the voice is coming from.

"Freiter Gali!" I say to one of my men, "go to the first lieutenant and ask permission to pursue the voice."[2]

Freiter Gali is a Magyar with the heart of a lion, who serves me with doglike devotion. He returns and says:

"The Herr Oberleutnant says we can go, if we wish to."

I leave a man on guard, take another man with me, and walk in the direction of the enemy line, after the voice. Thick darkness envelops us like a light, foggy rain. We walk hand in hand, so as not to get lost in the smothering darkness.

For the past three days, the front has been quiet: not a shot has been fired. Such silence is a little suspicious: it usually brings with it an unpleasant

---

1   Avigdor Hameiri, "Hanale," *HaShiloah: Journal of Literature, Science and Life* 43, Jerusalem, Tishrei—Adar, Tarpah (1923-1924), 109-114.

2   A cover name for *Gefreiter* (private first class or lance corporal) Pály, Hameiri's batman, described in his two war novels.

surprise, the calm before the storm. The silence is doubly threatening, because it feels like someone is lying in wait for us. The piercing voice in front of us is that of a woman.

A woman? Between enemy lines? A place where even a bird wouldn't dare alight? And now? In the middle of the night?

And in a cemetery?

It makes no difference. On the contrary, its very strangeness makes it significant. The silence penetrates the very marrow of our bones

"Shouldn't we go back?" I ask my friend.

Freiter Galy says:

"Certainly not. Firstly, it would be a disgrace and secondly, how can a red-blooded man give up the chance to go woman-hunting? One woman is worth more than all enemy monarchies combined!"

We walk forward silently, on tiptoe, ready to fall flat on the ground at any sign of an enemy rocket flare—then all would be lost.

The weeping stops for a few moments, then begins again.

"Perhaps we'll have the privilege of an enjoyable duel," Gali whispers, "a regulation duel, for the sake of the fair sex."

Silence. The voice stops, but then the weeping starts again, deep and full of sorrow like a bereaved mother lamenting her sons lost in the bloom of youth.

Strange: a Jewish cemetery in the middle of the night suddenly makes me a coward. A thousand deaths await in the enemy trenches, thousands of rifle barrels gape at me from only a few feet away. But this voice, coming from a Jewish cemetery, makes my hair stand on end.

We are now very close to the as yet unknown weeping woman. We can make out her dark figure: she doesn't move. Lighting a match is impossible: it's light would expose us.

I approach the dark shadow which lies in corpse-like silence. I creep one step forward and touch it. The shadow moves and suddenly grabs at my hand!

"Hell and damnation! Who are you?" I whisper and a shiver runs down my spine.

"A young Jewish woman."

"A young Jewish woman." That's good news indeed on the Galician front. After all, young Jewish women bring no corruption with them!

I have hardly finished asking her what she is doing here, when she gets up, rummages inside her bodice, takes out a piece of paper, and thrusts it into my rough paw. Without letting go of my hand, she suddenly starts to flee on tiptoe towards our line like a graceful doe, dragging me along with her.

At exactly that moment, several rows of rifles open up: bullets shriek above our heads. They must have felt something. The rifles only miss their mark by a few hairs. My companion's hat is pierced by two bullets at the same time.

"What wonderful marksmen these bastards are!' Freiter Gali says while jumping away, "a head is worthless, but the hat is worth money, God curse them!"

When we arrive at our line and are able to take a breath, I take a look at the piece of paper and my face becomes pale as a sheet. It's a map of the Russian Front, the like of which their enemy has never before held in his quivering hands. A complete map, with all the important places, reserve armies, quarters of all the senior officers, stables, quartermasters, command, cannons—everything in detail.

A detailed list of an entire division.

My heart starts to beat like an alarm bell (oh, what a soldier's heart!).

I look at my honored guest: a young dark-complexioned Jewish girl, tender, delicate, well-rounded, with a pale face and flowing, coal-black hair. Tears still glisten in her eyes.

She is very tired.

My hands holding the map visibly tremble. Who has grasped such war booty in his hand? What a find! Freiter Galy is right: What is any old general worth compared with this piece of paper?

"What is your name, my dear?"

"Hanale," she whispers modestly and embarrassedly.

After I introduce my honored guest to the colonel and hand him the map, his face, flushed with a bit too much wine, becomes pale. He looks at the paper, then at the girl, and then again at the map, and says warmly:

"Thank you."

He turns to the uninvited but welcome guest:

"Where did you get this, little sister?"

Hanale is tired and worn out; she hasn't finished speaking when the colonel asks:

"Where do you come from, little one?"

"From the Jewish cemetery!"

The colonel fingers the map a bit, examines it carefully, and his whole body trembles. The wine that he has consumed evaporates and he is a little embarrassed that the matter has made such a strong impression on him. He tries to control himself.

"What's your name, little dove?" he asks again.

"Hanale," she replies in a sing-song voice.

"Hanale, my dear, please explain this whole business to me calmly but simply. Please tell me everything you know."

Hanale summons up the remainder of her strength. In a voice still trembling with fear and nervousness, but also with tender grace, she relates the following:

"I had hidden away with my aunt. My parents were already dead, killed by the Cossacks last year. Now, when they returned and reoccupied our village, we hid from them in the attic. But we didn't have enough food and strength to stay. Hunger forced us to leave the attic, and a Cossack officer saw me when I was coming down and wanted to escape. He didn't allow me to run away, but didn't treat me badly. On the contrary, he tried his best to treat me with proper respect, and after that he started to say that he loved me. He kept on prattling that he loved me very much. I didn't answer him—but he still began to boast that, when he gets leave in a few days' time, he'll take me back home with him. I told him that I wouldn't go, but he continued prattling that he was the son of a rich landowner and that his family would treat me with respect and honor. I would forget that I was Jewish with them. I started to feel a kind of disgust and inner revulsion. That he would take me with him? Who heard of such a thing! And that I would forget my faith? Thank you very much, but no! Apart from that, I am not chattel that can be taken anywhere he pleased! I should be the wife of a Cossack? Never! And apart from that, I already have a betrothed."

"A betrothed? Where is he?" the colonel asks with a smile.

"He is serving in the army, somewhere on the front, I don't know exactly where: I think in the Sixty-Sixth Regiment."

The Sixty-Sixth is our neighboring regiment.

"What is his name?"

"Moshe Yosef Shapira."

The colonel indicates that I should telephone and ask; I ask him to ask someone else.

Hanale goes on:

"I have been engaged for more than a year. The engagement took place a few days before war broke out and he was conscripted. Who knew what would happen? We even fixed a wedding date. Who could have known?"

Tears well up and cover her dim eyes like a night in spring.

The colonel calms her down:

"No matter, with God's help the wedding will take place. When was the scheduled date?"

"On the twenty second of this month, that was yesterday. I always thought about this day. And now .. ?"

She bursts out into bitter tears.

"Now this wicked beast came, even boasted that he would take me on the same day. My blood burned like burning pitch. 'No,' I thought to myself, 'this will never happen! He won't get his wish! You animal in human disguise!' I didn't put my thoughts into words, because otherwise I wouldn't have been able to get rid of him. I told him I didn't hate him, but that he just disgusts me a little because the Russians eat Jews alive. He laughed, happy that I wasn't trying to avoid him and was making an effort to get close to him. He grabbed me and started to kiss and paw me . . . There was no one at home. I screamed—he was a wild beast."

Hanale falls silent and tries to swallow her tears. She covers her face and weeps.

"A terrible disgust took hold of my entire body, I hit and kicked him, but he just smiled. He told me that, no matter what I thought, I already belonged to him, because in two days' time he would travel home and I should prepare myself for the journey. I started to weep; I already had a betrothed. He told me that I was a fool: my betrothed had either been killed in the war or, if he was still alive, would surely die in three or four days' time, because the Russians were preparing a great offensive against the Austrians. Not one Austrian—not even a refugee—would remain alive after this offensive."[3]

We look at each other.

"When I heard what he said, my face blanched, but I tried to at least look calm. I thought of my betrothed, of my dear departed parents, and the kiss on my face started to burn like all the fires of hell. Shame and revenge took

---

3 During the opening months of the war through fall 1914, the Austro-Hungarians suffered numerous defeats against numerically superior Russian forces pushing into Galicia and the Carpathian foothills.

hold of me and I promised myself that I would flee. I knew that it wouldn't be easy. The village was surrounded by Russian guards on all sides. But I felt that it would be better to die a gruesome death than go with him. If I had to run away, it would be better to flee *here*, to my betrothed. Next morning, I saw him sitting at the table drafting something. I asked what he was drafting. I approached him without fear and he was pleasantly surprised. He replied with emphasis and pride: 'This is a very important map of the war, only entrusted to a very important, intelligent man.' He wanted thereby to emphasize how important he was, so that I would not regret it afterwards. My heart started to beat rapidly and I suddenly burst into tears. 'Why are you crying?' I myself didn't know why, but in the meanwhile a thought flashed into my mind: 'I won't cry,' I told him, 'and tomorrow I will travel with you to a foreign land. But I cannot leave without my mother's blessing.' 'Where is your mother?' he asked me. 'In the cemetery,' I answered. He shook his head. 'No, my dear, that is impossible. Out of the question! The cemetery lies between the two front lines and entry to it is strictly prohibited, even to me! But why do you need to visit her? You must forget that Jewish woman!' At that moment, it was if a dull, rusty blade had been thrust into my heart. He said: 'That Jewish woman'— my own dearly departed mother, murdered by Cossacks! I burst into tears and he tried to comfort me. He saw (or thought he saw) that I finally loved him and had gotten used to him, and would try to do what he could. 'I know,' I said to him, 'that if you really want to, you can do anything! I cannot leave my mother without her parting blessing.' He calmed me down and promised that, that evening, he would take me to the cemetery. That evening he would be on guard duty. If I wasn't afraid I could go, but only at night. I thought of the kiss and of 'that Jewish woman,' and vowed that I would take revenge on him! I stole a copy of the drafted paper and, that night, set out, fleeing like a crazy woman. I wanted to run here, but despite terrible fear my legs carried me to the cemetery, to my mother. I fell on her grave: all fear left me. I asked forgiveness for the filthy kiss which that pig had implanted on me against my will—by my life, against my will!"

She bursts into a fit of such bitter weeping that our eyes fill with tears as well.

"What kind of reward do you want for bringing us this map, Hanale?" the colonel asks.

Hanale dries her tears, thinks a little, stands up and says:

"The only thing I want is to see my betrothed."

In the meanwhile, the man returns from the telephone and announces that Moshe Yosef Shapira is a telephonist in the Sixty-Sixth Regiment.

Within the hour they bring in a young man with the typical face of a yeshiva student. When the girl sees him she closes her eyes. Total silence: nervous waiting. Then she raises her wet eyes and only two words escape from her mouth: "Moshe Yossel!"

The two young souls stand as if dumbfounded, looking at each other, two young, pale, frozen lovers, pale as whitewash.

This sight moves even the old general who has come in to see what is going on: tears shine his eyes as well.

"So go on—embrace each other!" says the colonel.

Hanale rises and suddenly falls to the colonel's knees, kisses his hands, and then falls to the ground weeping, weeping . . .

After a few moments, the earth-splitting thunder of thousands of cannons cuts through the thick foggy darkness and the glow of reddish-black fires arises from the village, reddening the horizon for miles around. From the midst of the flames and astonishing noise that shakes the sky, broken, heartbreaking death screams and harrowing agonal rattles rend the heavens. The shell and shrapnel explosions combine with the death cries to produce a hellish head-splitting, deafening tumult. We stand silently, looking at and listening to the terrible balls of fire. None of us say a word. Suddenly we hear the sound of silent weeping—Hanale falls to the ground, weeping bitterly. What is happening?

At that exact moment, something totally unexpected happens. Hanale gets up and walks towards the enemy lines, towards the flames, with thousands of bullets, shells, and shrapnel exploding around her. She looks for a moment with wide open, round, frozen eyes—and suddenly, when we call out to her, runs with all her strength towards the flames and fire, calling out in a terrible, hoarse voice:

"Dimitry Ivanovich! Dimitry Ivanovich! I'm coming! I'm coming! Dimitry Ivanovich!"

She disappears into the reddish flames and thousands of explosions hurling up dust and ash towards the heavens. We all stand like frozen devils, rooted to the ground.

Moshe Yosef Shapira looks around, then starts after her. He runs forward a few paces into the reddish darkness, trips on a stone, falls on his face, gets up, and runs after her with all his strength, calling out tearfully:

"Hanale! Hanale!"

He too disappears into the terrible maelstrom.

The firing and noise start to die down, the heavens burn, as if struck by a great reddish, burning blow. From the depths of the reddish fog, trembling before us like a curtain, we see the figure of a man walking towards us.—it's Moshe Yosef Shapira. He limps forward, dragging his legs, and sighs with silent sobs. When we approach him, he bursts into tears. His voice is strangely distorted:

"Hanah! Hanah!" the poor wretched man howls. He shows us something. "Hanah! Hanale! The ring! Woe is me, Hanale!"

He falls to the ground and starts to chew his hands, and tears his skin bloody. He convulses, groans, quivers, screams, and curses: "Franz Joseph the First! War! Bastard! Hanale!"

"He's gone mad!" An officer says and shoots him dead.

I approach the dead man. *In his wrinkled hand, he grasps an upper arm, amputated at the shoulder, clasping it to his face.* A small gold engagement ring shines on the amputated hand. I read the inscription on it and thrust it into the dead man's hand:

The words engraved on the ring, still shine before my eyes:

"Hanale—Moshe Yosef Shapira, the 22th of Av, Tar'ad (1914). Mazal Tov."

Matrimony[1]

Death jubilation crowds fume,
prepared is your pale groom,
heaven's canopy extended above,
come, my orphan, marry me, love.

Our crimson carpet: thriving death pasture,
festive banners surge high with rapture,
and the table is set with cadaver decay,
come, my orphan—for you they all wait.

Our faithful guests—scavengers, birds of prey,
our minister—death, lord of dismay,
and thousands of cannons cheer loud, blood red,
come, my orphan—to thee I wed.

---

1   Avigdor Hameiri, "Klulot," *Ta'am Mita, Ha'olam* (Berlin), July 2, 1923, 8.

A Night of Vigil[1]

1.

"I'm telling you the truth, my friend," the new major, who arrived in the trenches only yesterday, says to me. "I won't deny that I could have stayed at home, that is to say the barracks away from the front, for another six months but I didn't want to. I really am ill: my one lung is somewhat tubercular. As you know, my old father is an influential physician. If I had said one word of objection to him, I could have stayed at home and probably not come here at all. But I wanted to serve, so here I am."

"Is it the homeland? The scent of bravery that exudes back home from the front?" I ask, like one who tries to guess why he wants to serve here.

"To hell with the homeland's scent! I am not an ardent 'patriot.' I don't give a hoot for the whole business of bravery and homeland."

"So why then? The life here . . . the nervous tension . . . why?"

"You're right. You've predicted it without knowing why. There is only one thing in my life that has aroused me, but which I have never been able to enjoy until now. Do you know what it is?"

"I haven't a clue."

"*The face of a dead man*," the major says seriously. "Yes, faces of dead bodies. I have seen many things in my life, but one thing is completely foreign to me: I have never seen a dead man."

"How is this possible?"

"It's no coincidence. I am an only child and my parents are not Catholics, but Calvinists.[2] You know that Calvinists don't allow themselves or others to

---

1   Avigdor Hameiri, "Lel Shimurim," *Doar Hayom*, March 30, 1923, 8-9. Exodus 12:42, Pesach eve: "Because the Lord kept vigil that night to bring them out of Egypt, on this night all the Israelites are to keep vigil to honor the Lord for the generations to come." Can also mean a night studying Torah.

2   The earliest Magyars were Calvinists, not Catholics.

look at the face of a corpse. My mother was particularly careful with me in this regard, out of fear that I don't suddenly panic. That's the reason I have never seen a dead man's face."[3]

"What about in the theater?"

"I have seen it there, but that means nothing. I know that it's just a game and that in a few minutes the actor will get up and bow to the audience's applause. But a real dead man is a very important thing, my friend, and the feeling that I have seen one would change my life completely. Just imagine: you see a man that, only a few moments ago, ate, drank, and philosophized with you—and suddenly you see him lying motionless. You speak to him and he doesn't move or answer you. That must be really funny. . . ."

"I don't need to see it to imagine it. . . . But funny? I don't think so. Maybe a little ridiculous. . . . But funny? No. We have seen many dead bodies here, my friend, and have forgotten how to laugh."

"That's exactly what I want to finally see and feel for the first time. When will the enemy attack?"

The question of a real greenhorn—a naïve man who has remained in his barracks and now comes here for theater. In addition, he isn't a simple soldier: he's a major, an officer of high rank! "When will the attack come?" he asks . . .

"The enemy always forgets to inform us in advance when he will attack, Herr Major," I reply in my best official tone, but with a hint of anger at this disrespectful question from a senior officer.

It's midnight and we go to sleep.

2.

There has been no fighting at the front for the past four weeks. From time to time a rain of hot shrapnel and a sudden hail of bullets falls. But these don't reach the levels of the real war that we have experienced previously. Both we and the enemy are prepared. After the first great snow and the mud that exhausts body and spirit . . . then it will begin again.

This state of affairs annoys the spoiled Herr Major. It's a real catastrophe. He has been at the front for several days, but only arrived at our position yesterday. We are the forward scouts, the "first line of defense." Experience of death has not become "therapeutic" for us.

---

3   The origin of this statement is unclear.

The major walks around agitated all day, apparently for no reason. We sense no fear in him, and yet he gives the impression of being on edge. But now that he has revealed his secret to me, I understand. He is longing for the dead.

We both soon fall into a deep sleep: he falls asleep first, and I hear him mumbling and stammering in his sleep. It is difficult to make out what he as saying, but a few disconnected words are audible:

"Rab Zalman Ber—a religious Jew—in death—there is no death—you are a swindler—a Jewish swindler—you are the . . ."

He laughs in his sleep.

I fall asleep as well.

After some time has passed, he wakes me up.

"Excuse me . . . Please excuse me . . . How . . . I have something to ask of you."

"At your command, Herr Major."

"No, no. Not officially, but as a friend. You are a more experienced officer than I, even though I hold a more senior rank."

"At your command, Herr Major," I yell angrily: he has woken me up for nothing.

"Don't get angry about something personal and nonofficial, please."

"If you please."

"I have given our artillery company the signal to attack."

"Have you gone mad?"

"Shhh . . . it has been done. I have given the signal. Why are you so upset? I have permission to do this."

"You don't have permission to send all our souls to hell!"

"All? Why all? Ridiculous. We'll 'take cover' here and you send these five men to the foremost 'protected' vantage point . . . Only they will be in danger."

"That is . . . that is . . . that is . . ."

"I know that it is an abomination." The major's voice suddenly turns serious and very grave. "But I take personal responsibility for what I have done! Do you understand?"

"I understand, sir."

I get up and send my five men to the commanded spot.

Quite obviously, I don't go to sleep again after that. The order states that we will attack the enemy tomorrow evening. In other words, tomorrow evening our first line of defense will be destroyed like Sodom and Gomorrah, with the five men in it. They will all be blown to pieces.

I am lying on my bed when suddenly there is a knock at the door. Rav Zalman Ber, the oldest soldier in our battalion, enters, an earnest request written all over his face:

"Sir, I want to be with my sons tomorrow night."

"How many sons do you have?"

"Four."

"Where are they?"

"They are all under your command, sir."

"What are their names?" "Their names? They are all different. One is called Avraham Kilini, the second Shlomo Kalvari, the third Moshe Karas, the fourth still has his old name—Michael Kohen."[4]

"So Kilini, Kalvari, Karas, and Kohen are all your sons?"

"Yes, sir."

Devil knows what all this means. If their father is Kohen, how can they be Kilini, Kalvari, Karas, and Kohen? Nu, thank God at least one of them remains a Kohen.

"Why do you want to be with your sons tomorrow evening?"

"Tomorrow evening, sir, tomorrow evening. . . . Please be informed, sir, that tomorrow evening is one of our festivals: Pesach," the old man says, smiling apologetically. . . .

"Aha . . . the 'seder.'[5] Nu good. Why not? I can permit you this enjoyment. Why not?"[6]

It's as if an axe strikes my head and my heart leaps into my throat.

"Hell and damnation! They are all at the 'protected' vantage point! I sent them there a few moments ago, at the Herr Major's command! I am not guilty!" I justify myself to the ordinary soldier. I am truly not guilty. Why didn't someone tell me that they were all brothers?" "It doesn't matter . . . it doesn't matter . . .," the old man stammers, his face pale. "It's not important . . . it's not important, sir. We are not cowards . . . I am an old, experienced soldier . . . On the contrary, it's very good for them to all be together . . ."

---

4   The reason for different surnames starting with the same letter is unclear.

5   Ceremonial meal on Pesach eve commemorating the Exodus from Egypt.

6   Hameiri wasn't an observant Jew, so he might not have known the exact date. In *Hell on Earth*, he is unaware of Pesach dates as well (see Avigdor Hameiri, *Hell on Earth*, trans. Peter C. Appelbaum [Detroit, MI: Wayne State University Press, 2017], 385-386).

"Wake up, man! In the forward vantage point, they serve as cannon fodder!"

"So what? ... Good ... I will be with them as well."

"That's all they need there! It's impossible!"

The old man's eyes overflow with tears.

"Honored sir, I implore you—you know what a seder is. I am an old man—never in all my life have I led a seder without my sons ... Hashem[7] will repay you with blessings, honored sir."

My heart convulses.

The old man feels this and comforts me with a smile.

"It doesn't matter, sir ... Pesach eve, the night of vigil ... place your faith in the Lord, sir ... there is no danger on the night of vigil ... the Jewish God ... I implore you."

"Where have you come from, in the middle of the night?"

The old man stammers for a moment, walks back and forth, swallows his spittle, and says:

"Excuse me, honored sir ... From there. I was with them ... I stood watch until midnight. Then, when I heard that they had been sent there, I went to visit them ..."

To go "there" without orders is strictly forbidden—but I can't upset the old man ... father of four sons ... he wants to hold the seder with them ... let someone else try to stand against such a request and not allow it.

"Fine. Go to sleep and you can go there tomorrow."

As soon as the old man leaves the major wakes up, laughs, and rubs his hands with glee. "Wonderful. Just wonderful!"

3.

The evening of the day after, Pesach Eve tar'ah,[8] there is a commotion between the two lines. No fighting is taking place, but bullets reduce rocks to white powder and trees to stumps, and the rattling tears our nerves into pieces of cotton wool. Our minds feel nothing anymore: they are completely stupefied by the noise. Our brains feel as though they are being struck by a dull mallet,

---

7   Name for God in everyday parlance, especially used by Orthodox Jews.

8   March 29, 1915 (12 Nisan, 5676).

causing them to block up uncomfortably, and we can't stand on our own two legs without leaning on a wall.

Several hours pass in this way. The father with his four sons is "there." Tears begin to drop from my brain to my throat.

After that—silence.

I use this time and run towards the vantage point with my last breath.

I feel that someone is running behind me: I turn and see the major smiling.

I am seized by terrible anger. I glare straight at him and hurl the following words in his face:

"It's all for nothing. They're alive!"

"How do you know that?"

I have no words to say, nor lips to speak, nor throat to utter them, but a single phrase slips out, as if on its own:

"Night of vigil."

I turn from him, to hurry there. The major thinks that I have stammered out something in anger and doesn't understand what I have said. We run into the long, protected trench that leads, like a kind of open cellar, upwards to the forward position.

When I stand in front of their "concealed position," a kind of strange, sweet faintness takes hold of me. Behind the door I hear:

". . . who has created the fruit of the vine."[9]

I open the door and, with a feeling of vengeful victory, let the major come in. "Please be so kind as to enter."

Five voices sing joyfully through the open door and words of devotion[10] spill out onto us: "Pour out Your wrath on the nations that do not acknowledge You . . ."[11]

---

9 Blessing over wine: "Blessed are You, O Lord our God, King of the Universe, who created the fruit of the vine."

10 The word *kavana* means devoted, concentrated prayer. It is especially important for the Orthodox.

11 Psalms 79:6: "Pour out your wrath on the nations that do not acknowledge you, and on the kingdoms that do not call on your name." This prayer is recited during the second half of the seder ceremony, when the door is opened to welcome Elijah the Prophet. It was the only chance Jews had during the year to secretly curse the non-Jews under whom they were suffering.

It's impossible not to burst out laughing. The father and four sons laugh as well, without interrupting their singing. The rickety table is set: tablecloth, matzoth, wine, bitter herbs, charoset . . . everything.[12]

The major is completely confused. So as not to reveal his shame, he laughs involuntarily. Suddenly I see him grabbing a glass of wine, lifting it up, and wanting to drink it . . .

The old man jumps from his seat as if bitten by a snake! He snatches the full glass of wine away from the officer, raises it up, and says:

"Sir, that is forbidden! That is the cup of . . . of . . . Elijah the Prophet, may he be remembered for good!"

He puts the glass back on the table, fills another, places it next to Elijah's cup, pours the wine in the first cup onto the ground, fills it up again, and hands it to the major.

"Please, Herr Major, you are our honored guest."

I understand immediately. Elijah's cup has become ritually "poured out" as a drink offering.[13] Next to it he puts another glass, fills the ritually emptied first glass, and hands it to the major. After that he hands a glass of wine to me and to his four sons.

"Lehayim, sir!"[14]

We drink and it's as if our eyes have opened. All of them are dressed in white[15] except for the sixth man sitting at their table: he alone is dressed in uniform.

The major looks at them with wondering eyes: his face pale as a sheet.

Only now do I see that he is falling down drunk. He empties his glass almost involuntarily and tries to put the empty glass back onto the table, but it

---

12 Bitter herbs, as remembrance of the bitterness of slavery in Egypt. *Charoset*: a sweet, dark-colored paste made of fruits and nuts eaten at the seder. Its color and texture are meant to recall mortar (or mud used to make adobe bricks), which the Israelites used when they were enslaved in Egypt.

13 *Nesekh* (Hebrew). *Yayin nesekh* (lit., "poured wine") refers to wine which was poured in the service of idolatry. The Torah prohibits drinking or deriving any benefit or pleasure (*isur hana'ah*) from such wine (Avoda Zara 29b). This is a difficult passage to interpret. The non-Jewish major has tainted the wine, making it *nesekh* and unfit for a Jew to consume; the father throws it on the floor so that Elijah's glass will not have contaminated wine in it.

14 To life.

15 Funeral shroud or sign of mourning and repentance.

falls from his hand. He mops his wet brow as if he has just gotten out of a bath house and wanders back and forth. He leans on me and stammers out a dim question that is not a question, rubbing his eyes:

"What's this . . . ? Tell me, what? Are they alive? Are they dead? No, I must be drunk . . . I am visiting you. Tell me, are they dressed in white or not . . . ? Am I mistaken . . . ?"

I try to stop him from falling and calm him down, with a feeling that some sort of danger hovers over us:

"Yes, yes, sir. They are in white . . . You are not mistaken . . . They are dressed in white . . ."

"What?" the major mumbles and starts to vomit. "What? Are they really in white? . . . Oy! . . . What's the matter with me? . . . Hold me up for a minute . . . Oy! . . . Why are they in white? Are they dead . . . ?"

The old father gets up from his "reclining position to the left,"[16] comes up to the major, caresses him, and, with the restrained words of an old father, says:

"Honored sir, please don't . . . please pull yourself together . . . He has drunk a little too much . . . No matter . . . It won't harm him . . . Nu, sir, cheer up in Hashem's name."

The major falls over. The old man picks him up and carries him on his shoulders.

"Ay, honored sir . . . that isn't proper . . . is that how you treat the master of the house when he welcomes you as a guest and honors you with a glass of wine? . . . That isn't nice . . . Dear sir, please pull yourself together . . . I am a really insulted . . . My wine is good Pesach wine."

The major lies with eyes closed and breathes heavily without movement.

"It doesn't matter," the old man says in a relieved tone. "If Hashem wills it, this will pass . . . The Herr Major will not leave our battalion." He bends over to look at the major more closely.

Something strange then happens. The major opens his eyes a little, then widely, and looks into the old man's eyes . . . He lets out a powerful, hair-raising scream of terror as he embraces me:

---

16 The traditional way of partaking of the seder meal and drinking the wine. For further details, see Eliyahu Kitov, "Reclining," Chabad.org, accessed June 2, 2022, https://www.chabad.org/holidays/passover/pesach_cdo/aid/1707/jewish/Reclining.htm.

"Save me! . . . Save me! . . . He's alive! Rev Zalman Ber! . . . He's alive! . . . He's a swindler . . . he isn't dead . . . He's just dressed in a shroud to swindle me! . . . Chase him away! . . . Oh—Oh—Oh!"

A strange fear of death makes him dig his nails into me.

Chills run down up and down my spine. The old man's rheumy eyes stare at us. The major says: "Rav Zalman Ber." . . . How does he know his Jewish name? Where has he heard it before? . . .

I immediately remember our discussion and his mumbling while dreaming last night.

The major lies stretched out on the ground, and again a mixture of wine mixed with blood and bile flows out of his mouth. His body droops and it stops moving.

When the doctor arrives, he diagnoses a fatal heart attack.

4.

The next day I ask the old soldier:

"Did he know you from before?"

"I never saw him before in my life prior to yesterday."

"But how did he know your Jewish name?"

The old man shrugs his shoulders:

"Who knows?"

Afterwards, immersed in his own thoughts and, without looking me in the face, he says:

"Poor man . . . Sir, I know what he died from. Elijah the Prophet's cup is a very dangerous thing . . . he defiled it. Poor man . . . I am not to blame, sir."

By Hands of Man[1]

By hands of man, by hands of man,
this is inferno. Hell.
In this inferno bite your skin
and choke your yell.

It is not the hunger, nor the filth,
nor the wounds, nor the pain,
for here the soul roasts on embers,
not your frame.

By hands of man. By hands of man.
Look in his eyes, shed no tears,
beg him not, suppress all sighs,
Lest he hears.

Lest he sees you
and callously whispers: "suffer much?"
Then—smiles, lights a cigar,
and goes for lunch.

By hands of man, by hands of man,
who assumes the role of the god he hates,
while He sits in heavens high, laughing
at man's fate.

(Captivity Poems—Penza, 1917)

---

1   Avigdor Hameiri, "Al Yedei Adam," *Ha'aretz*, December 3, 1926, 5.

The Storm[1]

An evening breeze showers colors and melodies of faraway, long-lost rest in the frenzied air above our heads and hearts. First Aid Station Physician Scheier and I sit in our dug out and talk of peace.

Of the peace from which we have been orphaned; of enchanting tranquility, of humanity, and beautiful culture—all lost and gone forever.

We talk and talk, calmly, sadly, with dimmed hope, closed eyes, sick and yearning love of life, and compressed lips.

Dr. Scheier is racked with impatience. He gets up and says:

"Ay, my friend! Sitting here and philosophizing is not for me. This forced idleness dulls the heart and drives a man crazy! The first aid station is rife with disease and here I sit, wasting time talking about peace!"

Dr. Scheier has only been at the front for two weeks. Before this time, he worked at the city military hospital, devoted to his patients. He is only twenty-four years old, but his hair is already starting to turn gray. His health is not robust at the best of times, but the little strength that he has is dedicated to treatment of the terrible infectious diseases that ravage soldiers in this war. Even before qualifying, as a young physician's assistant, he had already worked wonders.[2]

Despite this, he is looked down upon by people in the city. The war has been raging for over a year already—and he is enjoying the good life at "home" and not at the front.

"He prowls around here," they say, "instead of going out to where the real war is, to protect the homeland!"

---

1   Avigdor Hameiri, "Sa'ar," *Hatoren* 10, no. 7 (December 1923), 96-101.

2   After Louis Pasteur (1822-1895) definitively showed that infectious diseases were caused by infectious bacterial agents, Robert Koch (1843-1910) pioneered their isolation and culture, and Paul Ehrlich (1854-1915) discovered arsphenamine for therapy of syphilis, the German-speaking world was at the forefront of microbiology and infectious diseases. Paul Ehrlich and Ilya Mechnikov (see below) laid the foundations of immunity as we know it today.

Dr. Scheier is continuously confronted with this muttering behind his back but doesn't have time to notice it because of the infectious diseases raging in his hospital, of which he is a mortal enemy.

To tell the truth, there is something about Dr. Scheier's face that turns people off and makes them uncomfortable. Perhaps it's the horn-rimmed spectacles perched on his odd-shaped nose, perhaps his lips which are a little too thick to be pleasing.

Maybe all of the above make Dr. Scheier unloved by everyone except the dangerously ill patients entrusted to his care. They love him much more than his commanding officer, His Excellency the Colonel, the exalted Herr Ober-stabsarzt.[3] His Excellency doesn't like to soil his hands with sickness, suffering, and sighs. He finds infectious diseases distasteful and his assistant Dr. Scheier most distasteful of all. Every chance he gets, he says:

"If I were still young and a bachelor like you, I wouldn't be as scared of danger, war, and the front as you are. Apart from that, I've already been there and you haven't. Strange: a young, cowardly bachelor. . ."

Dr. Scheier certainly is strange, young, and a bachelor, but he is certainly no coward. Danger stares at him with bloodshot eyes here no less than the seriously ill patients under his care and the tens of thousands of soldiers on the front, not to mention his own colleagues, who have recently died of infectious disease one after the other. Despite this, the Herr Oberstabsarzt casts an evil eye on him. "A soldier who wears His Majesty the Emperor's uniform should go out to war against the enemy."

Dr. Scheier has been sent to the front.

The only thing that he regrets is being forced to leave the poor patients in his hospital, swamped with loathsome infectious diseases. But no matter, there are plenty of patients who need his help at the front as well, and at least there they won't gossip behind his back. He will finally be in the midst of war, a place where everybody is regarded a hero.

Dr. Scheier harbors no hate towards anyone or anything in the world, except the miserable microbes. It's only against them that he wages war with all his heart and soul. But, with God's help, he will get used to another kind of war and another kind of hate, and will get used to dressing wounds. He suddenly finds himself in the midst of "war."

---

3   Equivalent to the rank of lieutenant colonel in the Austro-Hungarian army.

But fate has a nasty sense of humor. A few days later, an order from above also sends His Excellency the Herr Oberstabsarzt to the front.

And so he meets Dr. Scheier again.

Even now His Excellency the Colonel is not satisfied. Dr. Scheier isn't right in the front line. The "first aid station" is about three kilometers behind the line in a small town to which the seriously wounded are brought and in which the reserve battalion is held.

It's quite peculiar: even here, those same wretched transmissible infectious diseases plague the camp.[4] Dr. Scheier has come in time. Again, he fights against these diseases with all his strength and again the senior surgeon looks askance at him: Dr. Scheier is superfluous here!

"He's still not in a front line trench!" His Excellency grumbles. "He's still not really in the war! It isn't seemly for a young man to be such a coward. A young man should have a stout heart. Cowardice in a young man is offensive and the front line is a place for young people."

Dr. Scheier's pent up motions begin to get the better of him and he becomes quite insulted: this is finally too much.

But he soon forgets about it. He cleans his horned-rimmed glasses with a handkerchief and buries his face in his beloved microscope. In his search for bacteria, the rest of the world disappears.

The one time Dr. Scheier really got angry was when the office sergeant interfered with his work and distracted him. That interference cost Dr. Scheier the lives of several of his patients. His quiet face reddened in fierce and somewhat vocal protest. That protest was not customary with him and instead of achieving its purpose it was met with a few chuckles. But the issue was sufficient reason to get him removed. After all, Dr. Scheier was only an assistant physician and the office sergeant was considered to be the hospital superintendent, with an entire row of medals on his chest. His Excellency the Oberstabsarzt said to Dr. Scheier after the fact:

---

4   Transmissible infectious diseases caused great morbidity and mortality during World War I. Unsafe water supplies and sewage disposal systems in the trenches led to fecal-oral infections such as dysentery, typhoid fever, and cholera. Droplet infections caused respiratory infections such as bronchitis, pneumonia, and tuberculosis. Wound infections, including gas gangrene, were common. Insect-borne infectious diseases such as louse and flea-borne typhus and malaria caused great loss of life. There were no antibiotics available, and penetrating abdominal wounds were uniformly fatal due to leaking of bowel contents and peritonitis. The science of virology was decades away.

"Dear Scheier, lower your voice a little when speaking to this man. You have just got here and not served at the front yet. And this man . . . Look well on him, look at his chest . . . After time has passed, after you have experienced a few 'storms,' you'll be able to raise your voice. But for the moment, please lower it an octave."

Dr. Scheier lowered his voice so much that he stopped speaking completely. But in the meanwhile, he began to think about the strange fact that this sergeant had caused the death of many soldiers, including those serving in the front line. And yet they spoke of him with honor: even His Excellency the Herr Oberstabsarzt did! What good are medals in a field hospital?

Dr. Scheier reflected and realized that even his insignificant self didn't waste his life in idleness and that he wasn't completely superfluous. Even he had done some useful things, even he was, quite apparently, a human being. He straightened himself up, put his glasses on his nose, placed the medicine bottle properly on the table, and said:

"Excuse me, Your Excellency . . . excuse me . . . It seemed to me . . . I thought . . . I assumed . . . that death doesn't reside in places where decorations and respect gleam. One cannot purposely forget that accursed small microbes are tens of millions more than the enemy's bullets . . .[5] When I treat one infectious disease or another, I put my life in danger no less than any sergeant in the world."

Dr. Scheier's hard words seemed mad and ridiculous at the same time. Neither he nor anyone else had ever heard words like this out of his mouth. The physician in chief didn't reply. Instead, the order came: "Dr. Scheier— to the front line trenches at once!"

Dr. Scheier could speak like this there if he liked, bent over double to evade enemy bullets.

Yet again, Dr. Scheier only regretted one thing: that he was forced to leave the small town field hospital behind the front, with its cholera patients writhing in agony.[6] There is a kind of comfort, a sad glory, in a wounded soldier—

---

5   During World War I, the relatively long time that elapsed between wounding and treatment meant that many wounds were already infected by the time they arrived in dressing stations and field hospitals. Men sometimes lay in no-man's-land for several days before being removed for treatment.

6   The word cholera derives from two Hebrew words: *holi* (disease) and *ra* (bad, evil)

at least so it is thought. But a patient with an infectious disease suffers all the torments of hell.[7]

So, Dr. Scheier finds himself with us in a frontline trench.

But again, fate turns her adulterous face on him. There has been no fighting for several days and he sits idle. When we see him hiding his face in shame, we feel really sorry for him.

"I am going mad, my friend . . . Back at the 'first aid' station millions of microbes crawl around, rejoicing, being fruitful, and multiplying[8] with no let or hindrance. And here I sit, waiting for a bullet to wound someone."

He bends over me, saying:

"I'll return to the 'first aid' and reserve station. I hear that a new plague has broken out there and is killing the poor wretches."

"How can you return without authority or a command from above?"

"What do I care about authority or orders from above or below?" The young Jew becomes excited and his pale face reddens with innocent, self-righteous anger. "Authority or command—there are only two physicians there. The senior physician is His Excellency the Oberstabsarzt and his deputy doesn't even know how to dispense aspirin: he is a medical student with one year's experience. You know His Excellency, a 'family man with sons' who doesn't particularly like soiling his hands with infectious diseases. Whenever we visit a dangerously sick patient, he orders me to open the door—he doesn't even want to touch the lock . . ."

My warnings don't help. Dr. Scheier returns to the first aid station without authority or orders from above.

When he arrives in the small town, all the humble houses start to weep. The entire company hovers between life and death. Dr. Scheier finds no doctor there, just the medical student. Only two official people are working there: the Feldrabbiner and the Catholic priest doing their rounds, burying the dead in a continuous line, one after the other. The civilians who still have the strength go out with their hands on their heads, trying to touch nothing. All Dr. Scheier hears is weeping and prayer. His heart flutters and his whole being is taken up with wild, feverish work.

---

7   Untreated, bacterial infections diseases become septicemic and fatal.

8   Genesis 1:28.

That evening, thunder strikes the entire company: His Excellency the Commandant is coming![9] Without any prior notification or orders of the officers' intentions—a surprise visit. He goes straight to the quarantine house in which infectious disease patients are kept. He listens, with choked, restrained anger, to the official line that the reserve company doesn't have a single physician and that His Excellency the Oberstabsarzt has given an order, or better yet, permission, to abandon the little town and move to the nearest village in the rear.

The commandant reacts as if a snake has bitten him.

"What? To the rear!?" He roars like a lion shot by a poisoned arrow. "To the rear!? Accursed pigs! I'll hang you all on the same bare tree! All of you together! Give me pen and ink! Pen and ink, I tell you!"

He writes a series of death sentences.

All this is done in a few frozen moments that seem to those standing around in the room like a thousand years of damnation. All the soldiers on duty stand like tombstones, heads spinning like a top. Only one man in the room doesn't hear what is happening around him: young Dr. Scheier, sitting in his usual bent over position at his table, two blue daydreaming eyes immersed in his microscope. He hears neither the office sergeant's thundering yell of respect at the commandant's arrival, nor the Herr Oberstabsarzt's infuriating order or the commandant's angry roar—nothing. He sits at his microscope, cleans, adjusts, raises and lowers the glass slide and the lens, adds fluids and pours them from container to container, and looks again into his beloved microscope, which removes the curtain and reveals the formation of the terrible enemy: battalions of stubborn microorganisms that lie in wait, charge, twist, and reproduce. He doesn't even have time to see the commandant, who rises and asks with a flushed face:

"How are the patients doing at the moment?"

"At the moment . . . At the moment . . . The sergeant stammers with humility and a trembling fear of death. "Your Excellency, beg to report that their condition is a little better . . . better, Your Excellency."

"How many doctors did you say were on duty?" the commandant asks again, to make sure that he has heard the terrible truth.

"Only one, Your Excellency. Only one."

---

9   There is no exact English translation for "divisionary." The Austro-Hungarian army had no rank of brigadier, so the term is best translated by commandant.

"And who is he?"

The evil beast arises in the sergeant. He looks at Dr. Scheier and says:

"Dr. Scheier, the senior physician's deputy." In order to rob Dr. Scheier of his moment of glory the sergeant adds emphatically: "He ran away here illegally, without permission . . . *he ran away from the front line*—before the 'storm.' Tomorrow an enemy 'storm' is scheduled."

The commandant forgets about the plague of infectious diseases, the dead, and all the world's microbes. Sparks fly from his eyes. "This is a company of mad traitors: one leaves the sick and runs away to the rear, the second runs here from the front line . . ."

He gnashes his teeth and yells furiously at the young doctor:

"Dr. Scheier! Dr. Moshe Scheier! Are you deaf or dead?"

The young doctor rises from his work bench and, as he is, with white apron and bare hands, approaches the commandant.

"Here I am."

"Have you run away from the front?" the commandant asks. The doctor doesn't even know how to stand at attention, according to military usage!

"As you say, Your Excellency."

"Do you know what the punishment for running from the 'storm' is?"

Dr. Scheier doesn't reply. He bows his head respectfully and stretches out his hands like one inviting a guest to his table. He says respectfully and politely, with civilian emphasis:

"If you please, Your Excellency, be so kind as to take the trouble to step over to this table."

The commandant looks at the humble doctor as if he were an idiot. His civilian nonmilitary "waiter-like" gesture in a man wearing the emperor's uniform is distasteful. He wrinkles his brow and a slight smile smooths over the restrained anger on his face. Scheier's innocent impudence so surprises him that he yields to his request and goes over to the table, as if to say: "Nu, let's see what this strange ill-mannered person wants." Dr. Scheier adjusts the glass slide under the microscope, makes another nonmilitary waiter-like gesture, and says:

"Please be so kind as to look into this microscope."

The Great and Terrible Commandant casts a suspicious eye on Dr. Scheier but deigns to look into the microscope. He looks and looks . . . A faraway, strange world unfolds before his eyes. In the beginning all he sees is a wide, greenish circle in which a multitude of white spheres float back and forth quietly, sluggishly and immobile, as in a deep transparent greenish sea. It is as if each sphere has a whitish eye in its middle. The eyes stare straight at the commandant, like round, curious, slightly threatening fish eyes.

"What's this?" asks the commandant in a quiet but inquisitive voice.

The circle becomes smaller and smaller. The spheres become smaller but multiply: into thousands, into tens of thousands, into tens of millions.

"These are our battalions, Your Excellency," Dr. Scheier says calmly. "They are the defenders of our life's blood, standing watch on the battlefront of our bodies against future distress."

The picture changes again. The innumerable spheres transform into one large sphere whose one eye in the middle of its body looks straight into the commandant's eye. His head flinches a little.

"That is one of our faithful heroes," Dr. Scheier explains.

Suddenly the commandant sees a living image: a small, whitish snake approaches, coiling at the margin of the circle.

Dr. Scheier looks at the commandant's face and sees a grimace. "That's the enemy," he comments seriously.

The twisting snake approaches the sphere and spits out a blue drop, which flows straight into it.

"Attack. The enemy is attacking," says Dr. Scheier.

The sphere shakes violently and becomes alive.

"Aha! Aha!" His Excellency becomes excited.

A polypous arm with a hand protrudes suddenly from the body of the sphere. It surrounds and takes the snake in its grasp, clasps and squeezes it into the body of the sphere. The snake is swallowed, closed off on all sides, and strangled.

The commandant is very satisfied at what he sees. However, in the meanwhile the original snake has given birth to a second one, which does the same as the first. It ejects a poisonous drop and twists. But the arm stretches out and closes it in. The second snake gives birth to a third, a third and a fourth. Each multiplies and divides, giving rise to uncounted progeny. But polyp-like arms appear from the circle on all sides with blinding speed and cunning intuition. The circle swallows all the snakes, macerates and kills them instantaneously. What is left of the snakes freeze: they become dead carcasses and slowly dissolve. The circle returns to its previous state, floating calmly in its green sea, gradually digesting what is left of the snakes. One after the other, they disappear completely.

"Victory," says Dr. Scheier. "Onwards, if you please."

The white circle lies motionless. Suddenly, small snakes attack it from all sides in their hundreds, thousands, tens of thousands. They multiply second by second and spew rapid, deadly drops into the sphere continuously and angrily. The sphere puts out its arms on all sides, snatches, imprisons, closes, swallows, and macerates. But a mighty camp of snakes spew out venom; they shed their skin, twist, run to and fro. The sphere is already full of arms and so full of snake carcasses that they cannot be digested anymore. The snakes are fruitful, multiply unceasingly, and attack the sphere. The sphere defends itself and absorbs them one after the other, but in vain. The snakes are too many to all be swallowed, the sphere's arms become weak and tired, falter, and lose their strength.

The commandant turns to Dr. Scheier with a sudden head gesture.

"Don't let it happen! Don't!"

Dr. Scheier smiles and says:

"It's still alive. Help will come very soon—please continue looking."

He drops a type of fluid onto the glass under the lens. The commandant sees: a new, red stream suddenly flows on the left side of the circle and widens, creating increasing waves. The waves surround the circle which, when they reach it, is still wrestling with the snakes. The stream washes away the remaining snakes and, as if hit by a mighty blow, they steadily weaken. They suddenly freeze and try to escape, but cannot writhe anymore. The sphere recovers and sends out its arms again: they surround the weakened snakes, which are swallowed and sealed in. In the meantime, the snakes stop reproducing, become fewer and fewer, and disappear inside the body of the circle. After finishing its meal, the circle floats peacefully again inside the quiet greenish water, which, spits out bits and pieces of the evil snake carcasses...

His Excellency breathes a sigh of satisfaction.

"Now, with your kind indulgence, Your Excellency, now the 'storm' will break loose."[10]

"What will break loose?" the commandant asks.

---

10 Possibly modelled on the saying by the poet and soldier Theodor Körner (1791-1813) during the Napoleonic Wars: "Nun Volk steh auf und Sturm brich los" (now people rise up, and storm break loose). Infamously used by Goebbels in 1944 during his "total war" speech.

Dr. Scheier prepares the glass slide and suggests that the commandant looks into the microscope.

"The storm, Your Excellency."

A cruel picture unfolds. Uncountable spheres and even more snakes float around, as if in haste and fear. They sprawl over and lock horns with each other, fight, strangle, twist this way and that, flutter, escape, and attack again. Those who are caught try to escape, spewing poison. Some multiply, others swallow, dissolve, and kill. The tumult intensifies. The spheres are all full of arms which grab, macerate, shake, and close. But their enemy becomes more and more numerous. The spheres are all full to bursting of carcasses, but the snakes still multiply. One becomes two, two become four, and in no time, they become hundreds and thousands. In vain do the spheres exert all their power. The last of their strength dissipates and they give themselves up to their terrible fate. They float motionless, begin to shrink, become smaller and wrinkled, and are carried away to the shore, to the edges of the circle. The waves throw them out and the lovely greenish sea swarms with snakes. The sea gradually becomes pale and loses its transparent hue. It becomes murky, dirty, and polluted. The snakes breed with pleasure, swarm, and multiply without let or hindrance.

"That is the face of death," Dr. Scheier says quietly. "Our death, Your Excellency. This is the 'storm,' the epidemic, and *to* this 'storm' I ran from the front."

The commandant raises his sunken eyes that had been immersed in the strange world that move him to the depths of his soul. He ponders innocently, almost in the form of an entreaty:

"Can these evil creatures never be conquered?"

"Yes, it's possible, Your Excellency. With a little will good will and a little courage, everything is possible. The great danger with these snakes lies when one of them sticks to your finger and you wipe your mouth with it. In a few minutes, this storm will rage inside your stomach, intestines, and blood. This is the storm."[11]

---

11 See note 4. Rigorous handwashing to prevent infections caused by transmissible agents was first postulated by Ignaz Philipp Semmelweiss (1818-1865). He was laughed at and ignored until, decades later, Pasteur demonstrated transmissible bacteria and Koch stained and cultured them on solid media. Fecal-oral bacterial infections may remain in the bowel or (typhoid fever and less commonly bacillary dysentery) spread into the blood. Cholera is caused by a toxin produced by the bacterium that paralyzes exchange of fluid and electrolytes, and causes death by dehydration. Enteric viruses are spread by dirty hands. As stated, virology was unknown during World War I.

The commandant looks at Dr. Scheier without moving. He closes his eyes for a brief moment, scrutinizes the strange young man and barks in a stern, military voice:

"Tomorrow morning! Military judgment! Understood?"

"I understand, Your Excellency" says Dr. Scheier. He wrinkles his brow and returns to work.

The next morning, when Dr. Scheier arrives to hear his judgment, His Excellency the Commandant himself affixes the Military Medal First Class to the young doctor's gaunt, sunken chest.

"Pfui! The sergeant spits bitterly. "You see how Jews make business out of everything? They even make a profit out of cholera!"[12]

---

12   This story is a metaphor for the process of bacterial phagocytosis. The circle is the blood, spheres are phagocytes, and snakes are bacteria. The red stream is the circulation bringing phagocytes to the site of infection. When foreign bacteria enter the body, circulatory receptors (including opsonins) attract phagocytes to the site of infection. These phagocytes consist mainly of polymorphonuclear leukocytes. The leukocyte nuclei are the "eyes" of the sphere. The phagocytes then surround and ingest bacteria, lyse, and kill them. However, phagocytes may be ineffective in overwhelming or systemic infections. Ilya Ilyich Mechnikov (1845-1916) first hypothesized that bacteria were engulfed and destroyed by phagocytic leukocytes. This phenomenon was first quantified by Sir Almroth Wright (1861-1947), who (wrongly) proposed it as therapy. Hameiri knew of Mechnikov's work (see Avigdor Hameiri, *The Great Madness*, ed. Peter C. Appelbaum, rev. ed. [Middletown, RI: Stone Tower Press and Boston, MA: Black Widow Press, 2021], 88). The issue of "stimulating the phagocytes" was lampooned by George Bernard Shaw (1856-1950) in his play *The Doctor's Dilemma* (1906). Snakes spitting venom are analogous to toxin-producing bacteria, like those causing tetanus and gas gangrene. Tetanus was largely prevented during World War I by vaccination, but gas gangrene was common in neglected wound infections. As stated above, cholera is a toxigenic infection. The word *twisting* might refer to the spiral spirochete that causes syphilis.

The Filth King[1]

The windows are grimy, the wall smeared with ashes,
the door is broken, all evil passes,
and swarms of crickets chirp in masses,
instilling within me hunger's dismay—
Farewell to you, brothers of songs and decay,
farewell to you, brothers of songs and decay!

The walls are painted with bloody cough,
A hairy-bellied spider climbs aloft,
and dry flies convulse to and fro,
and death-mice squeaks disrupt the silence,
praised be, abominations, we are companions,
praised be, abominations, we are companions!

Mortar ground mud lie in wait,
cheerful fleas above fornicate,
through cracks in the ceiling the rain leaks with hate,
and plague puddles deliver to my nose the stench—
Welcome, suffocation, all light in me squelch,
Welcome, suffocation, all light in me squelch!

Red slumber suddenly clouds my mind,
Vermin and roaches caress my hide,
while I lie forgotten, my soul subsides,
and dazed I murmur and peacefully sing:
All hail me, all hail me, the filth king,
all hail me, all hail me, the filth king!

(*Captivity Poems—Tomsk 1917*)

---

1   Avigdor Hameiri, "The Filth King," in *Mitzpe Almanach*, ed. Asher Barasz (Tel Aviv, Mitzpe Publishing House, 1930), 79-80.

Sarah Bänger[1]

> Because you have said, We have made
> a covenant with death, and with hell are we
> in agreement (Isaiah 28:15).

1.

When the early morning sun's rays shone on the frosty flowers in the white window next to the mortuary laboratory, Sarah Bänger jumped out of bed and called out to her co-researcher while dressing:

"Ludwig, Comrade Ludwig, how much material was brought in during the night?"

A voice was heard behind the door:

"Seven bodies."

"A small number," Sarah Bänger murmured to herself, rubbing her blindingly white flesh in the snow.

2.

A small number, indeed: during the past few days very little material had been brought to Sarah Bänger's laboratory. A month or two earlier there had been plenty of work. An entire series of towns and villages had sent their excellent material to Dr. Rabinski's laboratory on the banks of the Dnieper.[2] Entire camps of marauding murderers had filled the laboratory with hacked up bodies and skulls. Oh, there was plenty of material with which to work.

---

1   Avigdor Hameiri, "Sarah Bänger," *Haolam*, June 22, 1923, 19-21; June 29, 1923, 18-20.

2   One of the major rivers of Europe, rising in the Valdai Hills near Smolensk, Russia, before flowing through Belarus and Ukraine to the Black Sea. It is the longest river in Ukraine and Belarus and is the fourth longest river in Europe.

Dr. Rabinski had rubbed his hands with pleasure, the pleasure of a kind of research Übermensch.

"Nu, Comrade Sarah, I'll make a bet with you. If within the coming month we don't make a sensational discovery in our research, you can put a bullet through my skull."

He continued with happy, complete confidence:

"I feel that we are very close to our goal. The devil cannot hide in a secret place for much longer. We will search him out and remove the silver shroud from his face. We are adapting death itself for our own purposes: that is a very good sign. This is the first time in the history of man that damage caused by murder and pogroms can be turned to our advantage. Won't this entire catastrophe be worth it if we can finally discover the organ responsible for fear of death and uproot it from our cowardly lives!? I feel that we are very close indeed to our goal."

However, the veracity of this statement was not clarified and Dr. Rabinski didn't succeed in drawing his world-shaking conclusions. That same terrible being whom he wanted to coopt and use for his own purposes—the Captain of Death—played a joke on the good doctor and placed him on the mortuary slab.

During the days that followed, his brain joined the others from which his pupil Sarah Bänger was trying to extract the solution to the mystery for which the entire laboratory had been constructed: the mystery of the fear of death.

That same mystery for which Dr. Rabinski had hypothesized a special organ, which he conjectured was part of the cerebrum, connected by one branch of the vagal artery to the heart, the other to the stomach.[3] The unravelling of this mystery had been his life's work and the goal of his heart and soul for the past several years. However, lack of "material" had hindered his work. To draw the final conclusion, he required material that was very hard to find: bodies of people who had died by unnatural causes. Dr. Rabinski, that doyen of researchers, couldn't find even a handful of such cases in his Geneva mortuary and decided that this city was not the correct place to perform his scientific research.

---

3   In Hebrew *etzev hatoeh* is the vagus nerve, one of the twelve cranial nerves. Hameiri is sarcastically calling *orek hatoeh* the vagal artery, which only supplies the vagal nerve, not the heart and stomach, poking fun at Dr. Rabinski's hypothesis.

"High culture, civilization," Dr. Rabinski grumbled in mocking despair,—"the aims of culture are much too low, in the light of our work and toil. People rejoice just because they are not murderers—as if the whole duty of man is simply to 'be fruitful, multiply on the earth, and increase upon it.'[4] It's as if our goal is merely to expose ourselves in the street and not plumb the depths. Things have come to such a pass that the sacred peace which is currently conquering the whole earth will rob from us even the smallest ability to penetrate our souls' depth, to know ourselves.[5] Man becomes a flower, a plant, a vegetable, as it were, that flourishes in the sun and then withers in peace. Take Lake Geneva: its miserable, faded waters have given up their life force in recent years: not even one corpse per year! Our counterfeit culture is contagious—contagious, I tell you—it sails on the water together with our steam ships and rules them as well with its delicate but rotting spirit!"

Dr. Rabinski saw no alternative but to spit in the face of this Swiss "city of peace,"[6] and flee back to his home on the banks of the Dnieper, which *didn't* give up its life force, nor scrimp on human life. There, he established a research laboratory.

In the meanwhile, destiny provided him with an undreamt-of gift—war broke out. The passionate doctor's lust for victory ran rampant like a wasp in a sea of poppies. He was seized with a sacred fever to enlarge and extend his research, widened and deepened by war in an unhoped-for way. At a time when the entire world groaned under storms of collapse and cries of horror, two people worked side by side in a laboratory on the banks of the Dnieper—the Pole Dr. Rabinski and the Jewess Sarah Bänger. Both zealously felt that the entire point of this tumult was to give them the ability to solve the riddle that gnawed at their feverish brains.

3.

In Dr. Rabinski's eyes, Sarah Bänger was no longer the neophyte who had worked with him in Geneva for a few years. She had been the only one in medical school class who paid attention to his theories and understood him

---

4   Genesis 9:7.

5   Know Thyself (γνῶθι σεαυτόν), one of the three maxims inscribed in the pronaos (forecourt) of the Temple of Apollo at Delphi.

6   Headquarters of the International Red Cross.

enthusiastically and she had returned home with him. Her colleague-in-spirit, Dr. Rabinski predicted a great future for her in his field of research. Sarah Bänger's attitude to the bodies lying before her in the mortuary slab was unique. She was the only one who agreed with his hypothesis. This young woman not only stood the test and abrogated her weak human feelings in favor of scientific knowledge, but also influenced him significantly. At times when he himself had to overcome weak, feminine feelings—when his goal demanded hordes of corpses—she, Sarah Bänger, intuited that the essence of death was nothing but material for the autopsy table.

In the beginning, Dr. Rabinski suspected that the Jewess Sarah Bänger would only remain unmoved by the blood of non-Jews, but he was pleasantly surprised. When the pogroms started and the mortuary filled with heads bearing beards and sidelocks, Sarah Bänger appeared unmoved. At the most, a kind of strange enthusiasm grew in her when she was occupied with a Jewish body. Her fair face became a little pale—that was all.

"I can already see," Dr. Rabinski said to his friends, "how right Fourier's hypothesis was.[7] The future of all skills in the world is to give birth to their own particular expert, designated for this from birth according to innate character. This young woman is a natural-born surgeon and I am happy to have given her the key to unlock her talent, which is destined to produce great things."

But Dr. Rabinski was not privileged to see this. He cut himself during a postmortem and developed septicemia.[8] He died after terrible suffering and hair-raising screams, and Sarah Bänger was left to her research alone.

Sarah Bänger didn't lose her spirit of enquiry. As people around her understood it, she was not orphaned scientifically by his death. Quite the contrary: like an exceptional student filled with her teacher's doctrine, she carried on her warped research with such enthusiasm that the new government—whose aim it was to "build a new life on the ruins of the old"—began to provide her with financial support. Sarah explained her research and the blessings it would being to humanity, to the new government, which promptly acceded to all her

---

7   Charles Fourier (1772-1837), French utopian thinker.

8   This was how Ignaz Philipp Semmelweiss (1818-1865) developed his theory of transmission of infectious agents by dirty hands. The chief of pathology in his hospital died of septicemia after cutting his hand during a postmortem. Because his post mortem showed the same signs as those of mothers dying from puerperal sepsis, Semmelweiss deduced that in both cases infectious agents had been introduced into the body through dirty hands. Handwashing dramatically decreased the incidence of infections.

demands. A young woman who could relate to the dead—and the dead of her own people—with such sacred equanimity—only a blind man couldn't see how the goal of human happiness lay before her eyes every day. Such enthusiasm on one hand and self-control on the other! It was difficult to define where the cold intellect of the superior researcher ended and bloodlust began.

The disgusting suspicion that she was occupied with the dissection of dead bodies only for the sake of perverted enjoyment did not cross anyone's mind except for one. He was none other than the laboratory assistant Ludwig Furyon, whose entire upright, romantic life was fervently bound up with this young woman.

Ludwig Furyon was a foreigner who had fallen into Russian captivity on the killing felds of the Eastern Front with a heart full of revulsion for war, after having burnt out his youth in the enthusiasm of holy slaughter. Having arrived here coincidentally after having passed through all nine levels of hell, he was put to work as a chemist.

Ludwig Furyon was a Jew, born into an assimilated family. His grandfather was a masonic grand master and he was devoted to this faith of the future with all his heart and soul. His love for Sarah was filled with deep, dissonant sorrow that he was totally incapable of bringing into harmony. This beautiful young woman turned his upright life upside down. The strong, fearless, self-controlled character of the young scientist, working so continuously and diligently, filled his heart to overflowing. At the start he felt as if she had gradually repaired a sort of crack in his soul and replaced the emptiness of his mother, who had left him in the fullness of her youth. Nothing of his mother's presence had been left to him but a few Jewish lullabies, ignored by his father, relatives, and friends. It was as if all this suddenly returned to life in the proximity of the young woman. Maybe Sarah Bänger's tender, warm, pleasant voice was the cause of this, or perhaps her dark, dormant Semitic features burdened his own soul with blurry, ancient, biblical legends. Perhaps both together had a pleasant but resolute influence on his soul. But the fact was that, when he saw her standing there with her blindingly white, dazzling apron, hands reeking with blood up to her elbows, a kind of sharp, suffocating mist stung his insides and distorted his face so badly that he couldn't see. Such treatment of dead bodies with pale, shriveled faces and dull half-opened eyes burned him like a flame.

In the beginning, when Dr. Rabinski was still alive, this did not stand out as much. "This damn Pole is responsible for what is happening to her," thought Ludwig. "He is the guilty party and it's still possible to save her from his evil hands." If it was possible, he would save her. Did she not love him no less than he loved her? It was clear to him that, after she left this Polish lunatic, she would return to the way she was before she came under his spell. As soon as Rabinski died, Ludwig decided to finally take her away from this filthy place, back on the wings of eagles[9] to his late mother's home. However, a small incident turned all Ludwig's plans on their head and drained all his strength. The body of Dr. Rabinski—who had died after dreadful suffering—did not yet have a chance to cool down, when Sarah Bänger washed her azure hands and urgently ordered Ludwig:

"Put the doctor's body on the table!"

This, after half her teacher's life had been devoted to Sarah's talents and her future and he had treated her like a delicate strange bloom which would flourish gloriously!

Ludwig's face whitened like molten lead.

"On the autopsy table?" he stammered confusedly.

Sarah Bänger nodded, shaking her shorn forelock enticingly:

"Autopsy table? Autopsy table? How can I allow a brain like that of Dr. Vaclav Rabinski," she asked in a surprised tone "to become food for worms and go to waste without dissecting it first? How can you be so naïve, my friend?"

Her blue-black eyes flashed with a cold, tough smile, penetrating Ludwig's very core. This proud scientist did not tolerate objection. Ludwig even forgot to call for an assistant: It was as if the devil himself raised the dead doctor from the couch onto the table.

It was the work of only a few moments to saw open his skull and remove Dr. Vaclav Rabinski's brain from the cranial cavity. Sarah Bänger at once separated both cerebral hemispheres, searching for the secret that this same brain . . .

From that day onwards, it was as if Ludwig Furyon walked around in a feverish haze. Only one thing gnawed at his soul: What kind of person was this strong-willed, delicate, beautiful but strange woman named Sarah Bänger? Who confused and mixed up her two extremes—delicate tenderness on one hand and iron cruelty on the other?

Who blurred this difference in his mind? Who put him under her spell?

Was this coincidence? Or revenge?

---

9   Isaiah 40:31.

It was vengeance, vengeance by the terrible god of war who had temporarily blinded Ludwig, grandson of Shlomo Furyon, grand master of serenity and eternal good. He was dazzled by this Lilith,[10] hands foaming with blood and pampered, as by perfumed water, with brains and hearts of still-warm murdered bodies. How could he escape from this hellish trap?

God's vengeance was truly terrible.

But another thought gnawed at his tired brain. How could he, Ludwig Furyon, theoretician of a "pure peace," someone who had imbued many students with his happy dreams of the future—how could he be so powerless to influence and eradicate this evil influence? What prevented him from overpowering her perverted inclination—she, who loved him so deeply—and making her abandon her evil art, casting the entire institute and its surrounds into hell?! Was she not his beloved, his betrothed, his best friend, his partner and wife-to-be?

He himself was guilty because of his initial stupid thoughts and actions. Why had he revealed his love for her so soon? Why had he not waited until she had come to him, opened her heart, and revealed her love for him, as is usually the case in mutual love? It soon become clear that because she had loved him deeply for a long while, she should have revealed her morbid relationship, as well as her inner warmth and tenderness towards him, long ago. She would have lost nothing by doing this. On the contrary. But he lost everything by doing what he did—he diminished himself and ruined the possibility of a healthy relationship. This is the judgment of a woman's love, a woman's way—it's a very old story. He became smaller—a high school boy, a puppet, a slave, a small, weak creature subject to her every whim. He became her toy—unable to influence her by his personality. But perhaps—maybe . . .

A cursed thought, which his entire being shied away from, occurred to him:

"What happens if I die today or tomorrow? Will she calmly open my skull, remove and dissect my brain with saw and scalpel, using the same delicate, dear hands that now caress me?"

---

10   Figure in Jewish mythology as Adam's first wife, created from the same clay as Adam. The figure of Lilith may relate in part to a historically earlier class of female demons (*lilītu*) in ancient Mesopotamian religion. Lilith continues to play a part in modern Western literature, occultism, fantasy, and horror.

4.

Ludwig Furyon finally decided to penetrate into her heart of darkness and search out the intimate details of her nature. It was difficult for him to place her out of his orbit, his heart and soul, and observe her from the side, as it were. But he was able to glean at least something from her past life. It was true that, up till now, her past had not interested him at all, nullified by the stormy present. He learned a great deal by peeling away the layers of her childhood years. He found out that Sarah Bänger never knew her mother and that her stepmother didn't give her any room to breathe. Her childhood was choked up.

Her three brothers were gruesomely murdered during pogroms and she fled the country leaving her father alone in some remote village or other.

She loved her father deeply and tenderly.

Nevertheless, she fled, against her will. Four evil men spread a net out for her, continuously lying in wait for her beauty and her tender body.

She used a "yellow ticket" to attend university in St. Petersburg[11] and was required to undergo weekly medical examinations for venereal disease like any common prostitute. Doctors abused her mockingly. When the secret police found out that she was a virgin, they expelled her from the city and threw her into prison.

In prison, she—a young woman studying science at university—was beaten bloody.

Hunger led to some kind of terrible humiliation. When her female Russian companions saw this, they laughed . . .

Ludwig Furyon would never have imagined that these events occurred, but they gave him the hint of a solution to the wonderful but sad secret which darkened his mind by its magic and consumed his life. Only now did he understand the great revolution that had occurred in this country and remember the few fragmented words that he heard, as if inaudibly, from his betrothed's mouth, which he had not understood at the time. She had never discussed politics with him. She gave the impression of having a wealth of opinions, but hid them from him. When he asked her about them, she closed her eyes, compressed her lips, and remained silent. When he entreated her to say something, she smiled and silenced him with her kisses. Once, when she was distracted,

---

11   A yellow prostitute ticket (жёлтый билет) allowed young Jewish woman to reside outside
     the Pale of Jewish Settlement in tsarist Russia.

she let a few words slip out, a few frequent phrases which he didn't understand at the time:

"This war was necessary," she said, almost unintentionally but with bitter earnestness, bursting out in a wild laugh. "A powerful rebellion—an eruption—a great and general destruction—a sudden evasion of existing authority—a rebellion without purpose or reckoning—a great vomiting up of everything: love, counterfeit Christianity, rotten hatred, principles, blood, life, gods—," she said and burst into a wild laughter, then caressed his face, and added fondly:

"What can an innocent Freemason like you know, my dear?" Some people drink milk all their lives, others drink blood—milk is white and blood is red . . ."

She laughed again and her eyes filled with tears. He would always remember that. She was as beautiful as sweet death. He didn't understand her, but understood the meaning of her words— a great vomiting. He saw what was being done around him—the tempest of blood—the compulsion to fight for holy human freedom even if it meant drowning in blood. He understood the terrible confusion of a liberated soul that is soaked in blood.

Out of this mad confusion, a picture rose up before him, a colossal silent monument that blinded the soul—like a statue that a sculptor creates out of red marble.[12] A picture of Sarah Bänger, subsisting on blood and squashed brains.

He got up and rubbed his eyes.

Everything became clear.

He understood everything that *she*, Sarah Bänger, didn't know or understand and about which she didn't want to speak.

Once when he tried to explain how he understood her soul, she laughed and said:

"You, my darling, are nothing but an innocent European. The mighty scientific ideal towers above all foreign thought and self-criticism. As I understand it, what you imagine is a personal thing—more than that, it is *foulness*. I only have one aim—science. To reach the goal that my brilliant master and friend Dr. Vaclav Rabinski placed before me—no more. Dr. Rabinski was right when he told me that I am a born autopsy pathologist. I feel it. For me a dead

---

12   A hymn recited on Yom Kippur eve likening God to a sculptor ("Ki Hinei Kachomer").

body isn't dead at all. It is research material, for mankind's sublime goal that towers above everything. Can you imagine the havoc wreaked upon us by our accursed nemesis—fear of death—this power by which any unnamed person or villain with arms in his hands can subjugate us? It commands us to kiss the lash that will slice us in two when we wish to see the face of God. Can you imagine the heights to which we could ascend, if not for the worm of fear that hides in a secret place in our brain and directs our entire lives according to its will? Fear, only fear!

"'He who kills himself only to kill fear will at once become a God,' Dostoevsky wrote.[13] I have another solution: not to kill ourselves and the fear, but to find it and gouge it out; to search for that accursed worm and liberate ourselves from it! That is my life's work. The new government has decided to bring this great scientific project to fruition, to a degree that I couldn't have imagined in my fondest dreams. They have realized how talented I am and support me financially. I will not rest until I reach my goal which is not mine or the government's alone but the goal of all mankind. My aim is to lay a small tile, a keystone, in the coming new world. But my goal demands human sacrifices—which great goal doesn't demand human sacrifices, or require cruelty? But the two even out—loss is balanced by gain. I know that you were shocked and astonished at my complaint of a few days ago that the recent pogroms didn't yield the body of a ten-year-old girl for my research. You were even more shocked when they really did bring me such a body and I rejoiced, as if it represented a great treasure.[14] So who of us is right? That little body gave me more material than a hundred adults. She was not a child to me, but rather a revealer of secrets. I can imagine my dead mother on the autopsy table when I . . ."

Ludwig Furyon put his hand in her lips:

"Leave it alone . . ."

He thought a bit, looked deep into her eyes, and asked with emphasis:

"And your father?"

Sarah Bänger suddenly became pale. She closed her eyes for a few moments. After a while, she recovered from her confused ideas, rubbed her eyes, and stammered awkwardly:

"My father? My father? I wanted him to see the conclusions of my research, no more. But as a body on my table?—Yes.—I am nearing my goal."

---

13   Fyodor Mikhailovich Dostoevsky (1821-1881), *Demons* (1871-1872), part 1, chapter 3.

14   Psalms 119:162.

This was the first time he saw her confused. How sacred her confusion was to him! How pure, how innocent—how she belonged to him! He kissed her on the forehead and asked her a question whose answer he should already have known:

"What was your father's trade?"

"He was a shohet.[15]

Ludwig Furyon was revolted by this one word. He looked into his beloved's eyes, raised his eyebrows, removed her hand from his and, although unintentionally, moved his chair a little away from hers. This single word reverberated in his brain like a silent thunderbolt. His hands sweated and it seemed to him that he was dealing with an impure creature. An attack of nausea racked his body, he lowered his head to the ground, closed and his eyes, and compressed his lashes tight. He heard her voice again:

"What about your father?"

A short silence.

Ludwig Furyon did not move from his seat or open his eyes. He replied in a monotonous voice that could have come from a marble statue:

"My father is a supreme court lawyer."

"And his father?"

Another short but difficult silence.

"One of my grandfathers was a masonic grand master of "eternal peace and tranquility,'" he concluded mechanically and almost inaudibly that the other was a shadchan.[16]

Sarah Bänger chuckled:

"If that is so, we are a match made in heaven." Her voice rang in his ears and he collapsed onto the sofa.

When Ludwig Furyon came to, it was as if he was looking at a female carcass. A living carcass whose stench dripped out and filled the room to suffocation. He jumped up and left the room.

5.

From that day on, Ludwig Furyon withdrew and secluded himself. The loving feelings that had filled his soul and removed all depression began to mix with

---

15   Jewish ritual slaughterer.
16   Jewish marriage broker.

another feeling entirely—one of pity. A deep feeling of compassion filled his soul when he looked at beautiful, pale Sarah Bänger, intoxicated with the terrible ideal that killed all the life, laughter, and femininity that she had been granted in such full measure. From then on, he began to concentrate all his strength into one goal—saving her from this terrible place. New surroundings, new situations under new heavens, new people. All these would succeed in restoring her to her previous state—return her beauty and her life. Until he achieved this, he would have to suffer, wait, stand on guard, look silently, and observe her, get to know her better, penetrate her inmost secrets, and hope. His hope would surely be fulfilled. Because, at the end of the day, she was a woman, with a divine spark that could not be suffocated in great, ringing, phrases—her pure love for her father. A great, warm childhood love is powerful enough to create a spiritual revolution that radically changes one's outlook. Such love cannot coexist with a savage beast—her present life was a mere coincidence, secondary to that feeling of filial love which burst forth from her like a spring flower from time to time, almost reaching a level of sanctity.

She had recently begun to receive letters from her father. These letters demonstrably improved her spirit, at least as Ludwig understood it. She became sadder and he regarded that as a good sign. She missed her old father and awaited his arrival as if he represented redemption. She prepared herself for him every day. Although she became sadder and sadder, she waited and made herself ready to welcome him. She beautified herself: body, face, and clothes. When the dear old father came he must see that his daughter was hale and hearty, working persistently and with great diligence, and that her work was financially and scientifically rewarding. Every move she made reminded her of her father, even when she prepared her instruments and sharpened her scalpels and cleaned them by boiling. She did everything in honor of that dear old man who had cared for her throughout his life and hung all his hopes on her. These were all good signs. When he came, everything would change for the better. Ludwig would speak to him. Her father would explain everything to her. He would compel her to choose another path and leave this dreadful cesspool of immorality in which all its inhabitants were turned into decadent worms swimming in perfumed blood, craving dead bodies, in a world where only death ruled. It was true that she was influencing *them*, all of them, with her doctrine, with her diligence, her perseverance in these cruel studies, her *Übermenschlichkeit*, with her so-called sacred science—with everything. It was also true that she had told him she could picture her dead mother on her autopsy table ready for dissection.

But his hope was suddenly dashed and his world darkened. There was no hope or rehabilitation possible for this wretched creature.

His blood began to sink from his brain down to his legs. He saw only one way out of this dilemma. One small bullet and then—the end. Let her run amok in these lunatic surroundings to her heart's content—he would leave this mad world, epitomized by this wretched, cursed young woman. He would leave it all behind and she would rot with the other corpses in her blood-soaked slaughterhouse.

He took the revolver in his hands.

Suddenly his eyes were darkened by the terrible image of him lying on the autopsy table, her hands squeezing his suppurating brain, a serious smile on her face.

He hurled the loaded revolver against the wall. It exploded with a roar. Sarah Bänger entered the room in panic. When she saw his confused state, she burst out laughing. It was the laugh of cold steel. She went up to him and her voice became serious.

"Stupid man!" she said with tender seriousness, "I know all about the foolish things that you are doing. Aren't you ashamed of yourself? You are a man!"

Her voice changed into a jesting laugh.

"We have more than enough cadavers here, my dear," she said, stroking his head, "one more or less won't make any difference."

Ludwig Furyon recoiled like a snake.

"Sarah!" he cried with a hoarse moan, "you are completely mad! You are out of your mind!"

"No, Ludwig" she replied. "I want to teach you to be a complete man. If you are a chemist, you must finally learn the . . ."

"I know! I know!" Ludwig interrupted her. "I know everything!" he cried, and covered his face with his hands.

She came up to him, smoothed his anguished face, and gave him a letter.

"Here, read! It's a letter from my father."

Ludwig took the letter with trembling hands and began to read it feverishly. There was a terrible pogrom in the town—he was ill. He had handed the letter to one of the soldiers forced to leave the town by the murderers. He himself had no more strength to accompany them. His legs were failing—they hurt him terribly. The town was awaiting the arrival of more bloodthirsty murderers with horror and dread—who knew what would happen . . ?

6.

Another letter arrived the next day. Thank God he was still alive: the murderers had left the town. Ludwig read the letter uncomprehendingly. What was this? Her father wrote that she should continue her work with diligence and perseverance and not let anything get her down. She should stand on the watchtowers of science every day, in the hope of a brighter future. Her heart should not become softened, nor should she protect people from human sacrifice—all for the sake of science, human happiness, etc., etc.

He rubbed his eyes in vain. He didn't understand a single word. How could this be? *Et tu, senex?*

She stood looking at him with a discerning eye:

"Nu Ludwig," she said victoriously, "this innocent, upright old Jew understands me perfectly. And you the young chemist—aren't you ashamed of yourself?"

Ludwig examined the letter carefully. Yes, it certainly was her father's handwriting. She didn't write in Hebrew—she understood and read it, but couldn't write it. Her handwriting was also different, with a different purpose. But what was so strange about his letter? After all, he was a shohet— a man who earned a living by shedding blood, albeit with a religious blessing—who blessed God through slaughter. And Sarah Bänger was her father's daughter.

Ludwig was seized by terrible nausea. He saw only one way out—to run away as fast as his legs could carry him, to wherever he thought fit. To run away and die there, as far away from her as possible! The main thing was not to fall into the hands of that obscene woman.

More letters followed, almost every day. Each letter made it clearer to him that he had business here with. . . . He felt his bile rising to his very soul: even his saliva turned bitter.

One evening, when he was ready to flee, he decided to speak seriously with her one last time, using all means necessary. He didn't let her kiss him for a while: tonight he would let her. He would speak to her tenderly, compassionately, with love and pity. She was so pale, her eyes were so tired, she was sick.

All he wanted was to cure her. He would weep, spill his guts to her, explain her error to her, that she was ill, very ill. He would cleanse her hands with his tears.

He left his suitcase and entered her room.

He stood behind the door.

There was a light in her room. The door was unlocked.

He entered.

He beheld a strange sight:

Sarah Bänger was sitting on a chair in her night dress half-naked, leaning on the right side of the table as if she had fallen asleep while writing a letter. Her head rested on her right hand stretching across the table. Her eyes were closed. Her hand wrote while she was asleep, as if on its own. She wrote rapidly without stopping, at times dipping the pen in the inkwell.

Ludwig understood what he was witnessing.

How could he have not realized before how sick she was? It was as if she was sleepwalking.

He walked gingerly towards her.

He looked at the letter and everything became clear. She was writing in Hebrew, in her father's handwriting.

Even the style was that of her father.

The content:

"May God guide your heart, my dear daughter—work hard in service of the sacred scientific revolution and ultimate honor."

His whole body trembled with fear.

He didn't wake her up, but looked with eyes popping out, taking in each letter that her pen wrote on the paper. When she finished the letter, it was if her hand fainted. He looked at the letter and read a new sentence:

"Work, my daughter, work. Don't spare your old father, whom you love and who loves you boundlessly, and offer his body as a sacrifice for the betterment of mankind. Fill the earth with—blood. Fill the earth with knowledge as the waters cover the sea."[17]

Her old father's handwriting.

His writing style.

Ludwig recoiled and fled like a madman.

---

17   After Isaiah 11:9. "For the earth will be filled with the knowledge of the Lord as the waters cover the sea."

7.

He didn't have the strength to run away that night, but sat and cried like a baby.

He took a dose of bromide and slept with difficulty.

Early next morning, he was awoken by a light tapping on his door. Sarah Bänger entered and handed him a letter.

Not only did Ludwig not read it, he didn't even touch it.

He looked at her sickly face and said nothing.

Her bulging eyes wandered like two dead pearls.

Her eyelids were red.

That smile—oh, that terrible smile! Cold, sick, and deadly.

He turned to the wall and broke out in a fit of weeping.

Sarah Bänger approached his bed, stroked his face with trembling hands, and said very quietly:

"Stupid!"

The word so astounded and confused his brain that he fell into a deep sleep.

After a few hours he was awakened by a terrible, bloodcurdling cry. It was the voice of Sarah Bänger. Ludwig jumped off the bed and began to rub his eyes. The scream became worse, grating and terrifying, nearer and nearer. Sarah Bänger burst into his room, hair disheveled, eyes reddened, and screamed with a moan reminiscent of a slaughtered animal choking on its own blood:

"My father! My father! Ludwig! My father has come! Here he is! Come, I'll show you! My father!"

She grabbed his shoulder with great force and pushed him into the autopsy room.

The body of an old Jew lay on the table. His legs were cut off below the knee and his moustache and beard were coated with a dry layer of clotted blood.

Sarah Bänger pounced on the dead body and started to suck its dead lips.

Ludwig Furyon was the only one able to bind her in chains.

The Bereaved Mothers[1]

First mother:
    For years I nurtured them,
    my blood I drew,
    alas, for whom?
    For whom? What for?
Chorus:
    For war.
    Alas, for war.
First mother:
    Day and night, bliss and joy,
    they were my verve, my glee,
    God has bestowed them upon me,
    alas, why did he bestow?
    Why?
Chorus:
    For Ashmedai.[2]
    Alas, for Ashmedai.
Second mother:
    They were two, two boys,
    two stars. Two eyes.
    One aged twenty-two forever lies.
    And the other—the other: gone missing.
    Perhaps somewhere living?
    Ever since I search.
Chorus:
    In vain you search.

---

1   Avigdor Hameiri, "Ha'imahot Ha'shakulot," *Davar*, May 10, 1936, 9

2   Ashmedai (Asmodeus, Ashema Deva): the prince of demons or, in Judeo-Islamic lore, king of the earthy spirits (shedim, jinn).

Second mother:
>   Everywhere I search.
>   At home, outside, the city, the village,
>   in the yard, on the street, in the church—
>   Under the pillow, under the perch—
>   Everywhere I search,
>   all my life I search,
>   everywhere, for a single thread—

Chorus:
>   In vain you search.
>   He is dead.—

Second mother:
>   He is dead?

Third mother:
>   My three boys went with delight.
>   Went without fright.
>   They bade farewell.

Chorus:
>   Farewell?
>   Alas, farewell.

Third mother:
>   The first returned with no eyes.
>   Stares at me with no eyes.
>   Searches my eyes with no eyes.
>   Feels my face with no eyes.
>   Smiles and weeps with no eyes.
>   Alas, with no eyes.

Chorus:
>   No eyes.
>   Alas, with no eyes

Third mother:
>   The second returned with no chin
>   and no cheeks.
>   Wishes to kiss me, has no cheeks.

Chorus:
>   Kiss him not, has no cheeks.

Third mother:
> The third returned mute,
> safe and sound—and mute.
> I wish to tell him something.
> What is it, son, something?—

Chorus:
> Mother!—
> Alas, mother!

Third mother:
> Alas, mother!
> Alas!

Fourth mother:
> I had one, only one,
> precious as three, as seven—a thousand as well!
> Went to the front—returned a shell,
> torn, broken, pale, burnt,
> then the order came: return!

Chorus:
> Return.
> Alas, return!

Fourth mother:
> Second time he returned wounded.
> Broken head, sunken forehead.
> Back on the saddle—
> Back to the battle.

Chorus:
> Back to the battle.

Fourth mother:
> Suddenly, a letter took my breath:
> Mass grave, heroic death,

Chorus:
> Heroic death.

Fourth mother:
> Heroic death, cursed, cursed!
> Return my son, return the theft,
> return him mangled,
> return him shredded,
> return what's left!
> Return me what I gave,

where is he? Where? Where is the grave?
Where is the grave?!
Chorus:
Heroic death. Death of the brave.
Alas, cursed mother, death of the brave.
The mothers:
Alas us all!
The Childless:
It was you who kindled your son's pyre.—
It was you who fanned the flames' fire.—
Who cheered the dancing devil?—
Who incensed the Molech?[3]
Who gouged the wound?
Who gaped his mouth to murder's hymn?
Chorus:
You, you, you,
Alas, you.
The Childless:
You set the street ablaze,
which boiled and steamed—
Chorus:
You.
The Childless:
All of you wore the pure uniform of white,
and assumed the role of nurses—
Chorus:
You, you.
The Childless:
You beamed smiles of delight
while facing the death curses.
Chorus:
You, you, you.
The Childless:
You invoked the spirit to die,
you engaged stake with torch,
you have elevated the death sigh
to a song of march.

---

3   Molech, Moloch: a Canaanite god to whom children were sacrificed.

Chorus:
>   You, you, you, you.

The mothers:
>   Alas to us, all of us!

The Childless:
>   With the banner of death
>   you stormed sun's shore—
>   You were whores, officers' whores,
>   war whores!

The mothers:
>   Alas to us, all of us!

Chorus:
>   Alas you, you, you, you.

The Childless:
>   And now, cry not in vain,
>   bless you, mothers no more,
>   comfort shall break through the pain,
>   for your sorrow shall kill the war.

Chorus:
>   Your sorrow shall kill the war.

Gift[1]

Drink, get drunk, and vomit, and fall to rise no more (Jeremiah 25:27)

1. The Festival of Decomposition

The golden crown of a sun of cursed miracles spills over into the village of Schinkenovka.[2] Its repulsive, blinding rays begin to penetrate the bodies of the dead that bless the outside yard, atrophying the dried-up flesh and helping create a veritable breeding ground for hundreds and thousands of corpse flies, maggots, and plague-carrying insects and worms which become fruitful and multiply joyfully on their newfound hosts.

The nauseating, torn bodies have lain around the village streets like worn-out rags for the past five days. Yesterday's pouring rain, which lasted all day and all night, has liquefied the bodies into a foul-smelling doughy substance which spreads its stench far and wide. Dogs and cats surround the bodies but turn away from them in disgust. Vultures flap clumsily over the open bellies, feasting on the innards, so sated that they almost fall asleep on the job. Other than these, nothing living can be seen far and wide.

On the walls of the houses, split almost in half by Russian rifles, an edict proclaims to Russians and Poles in large letters:

> Brothers! These corpses must stay where they are until the upcoming festival. Do not dare bury or even remove them. Let them lie where they are, rot, liquefy completely. We will celebrate the Festival of Decomposition of the Jews, brothers! It will take place this afternoon at 1:00 pm at the Schinken Estate. There we will await our dear guest, our

---

1 Avigdor Feuerstein, *"Eshkar," HaShiloah: Journal of Literature, Science and Life* [Jerusalem, Nissan-Ellul, Tarpab] 40 (1921-1922), 15-24; 128-136; 203-213.

2 *Schinken*: ham. Sarcastic name for the village and baroness. Pork is strictly forbidden to Jews.

honored, acclaimed, precious mistress, our eyes and the dawn of our lives, Baroness VON SCHINKEN.

Our eyes are raised towards her in eternal thanks for her great kindness. In our seven-fold distress she has not forgotten the servants who rely on her—the citizens of the village of Schinkenovka and the farmers on her estate. The baroness herself had asked us to arrange this festival on her behalf. She sent me a telegram yesterday in which she allocates a large sum of money for it. When our redeemer Baroness von Schinken, may her majesty be extolled, arrives this evening, we'll welcome her with a large bonfire, on which we'll burn all the Jewish carcasses at the same time, together with the ones locked up in our jails that we haven't finished off yet. We'll burn them all on the same altar and they will be turned into fertilizer.

Signed: Dr. Domshivski

Dr. Domshivski is the village and estate doctor, about forty-five years old. He is known for only one thing. He was imprisoned for six consecutive years in another country for something quite strange. He fell in love with the local beauty, Baroness von Weisenheim, in some small Swiss town or other. But when he despaired of finding a response to his desperate passion, he performed a small cosmetic operation on her eyes, blinding her for life.

Dr. Domshivski is now the animating spirit of the estate and village farmers who, according to advice from him and the Baroness von Schinken, are preparing the coming splendid Festival of Decomposition. He encourages their preparation for the magnificent occasion, explaining details of their war against the Jews and the role of the munificent baroness in this great victory. When the Jews conquered the country the baroness fled. Since then, she has become a stateless wanderer who has suffered greatly. She has no real need for this estate, which the Jews have defiled. As is well known, the baroness is rich and has estates and possessions aplenty outside the country. Wherever she finds herself, she is at home—a true citizen of the world. But her faithful, tender heart pines for her dear countrymen and coreligionists back home, and the good farmers and citizens of the village and estate. This is the reason that she suffers so terribly on their behalf and is doing so much for them. It would be a sin for Dr. Domshivski to withhold the manifold sacrifices that the baroness has made for her dear brothers and sisters. She has not even spared her own money, in an effort to convert General Nalivkovitz to their cause and recruit regiments to save them from the evil designs of the Jews. She has sacrificed one of her most expensive and treasured ornaments in an effort to collect a petition to Minister von Goredenz, who is exerting all his influence on behalf of his wretched countrymen groaning under the yoke of Jewish oppression. The dearly beloved munificent and exalted baroness has done all these things and many, many more on their behalf. She has even sacrificed her beauty—yes, yes, her tender and exalted grace itself—on the altar of their sacrifice. The brothers and sisters surely know of the catastrophe that has befallen the exalted baroness during recent days—the burn on her face. It is quite obvious that the Jews have perverted the truth about this. They have distorted the facts according to their evil minds and mocked her. They say that the burn was caused by another woman, the wife of a famous general, who threw a container of vitriol on her face out of jealousy for her husband. Is that not always the Jews' way—to defile everything sacred and exalted with their evil, lying mouths? The doctor has relayed the unalloyed truth to them. He knows that the courageous baroness endangered her life to save the homeland. She found out that the Jews outside the country were preparing to assassinate the splendid general. She risked her life by attending one of their secret meetings to spy on their activities. The cunning Jews almost killed her by placing a deadly moth on her face, horribly burning half of her beautiful face.

Yes, our brave baroness has done all these things—everything for her dear estate farmers and village citizens!

Therefore, every possible kind of thanks is due her for her courageous deeds, in this sad, unfortunate world!

The doctor knows that the brothers and sisters express their grateful thanks to their baroness from the depths of their hearts. Now, on her return to her estate, they owe her some sort of gift—how much more so when she herself has asked them to arrange a celebration! But it isn't so easy to find a suitable and appropriate gift for her, to express their thanks. Money? No, she already has gold and silver enough! What other kind of gift could they find for her? Difficult, very difficult. They have all been thinking about this for several days. The farmers, workers in the estate, at their head Dr. Domshivski and the army officers—who have delayed their military victories deliberating in the palatial estate—all have tried to find an exceptional gift to honor the baroness.

But Dr. Domshivski has not labored in vain his entire life on behalf of his brothers and sisters! Now, in their hour of need, he gives them a practical demonstration of his devotion.

After days of effort and exertion, the esteemed doctor has come up with a suitable gift for the dear baroness.

When all the preparations have been made and everything is ready for the festive meal, and everyone is somewhat sozzled with different types of liquor, Dr. Domshivski turns to his loyal brothers and sisters and says, in a wine-soaked voice:

"Brother and sisters, the noonday bell has already sounded. Half the day is passed and we will soon have the honor of welcoming our never-sufficiently-to-be-praised mistress. I know that all of you want to present the baroness with the most suitable gift and greatest tribute, as befits her noble spirit and many kindnesses. I know that all your eyes are directed on me, to advise you on this matter. You have not entrusted this thorny problem to me in vain. After much thought and effort, I have hit upon something most suitable. Brothers and sisters, you know the baroness's upright heart and her relationship with the Jews. You know of her constant efforts to bring these murderers who drink Christian blood without let or hindrance to the attention of the government and to proper justice. You all know the baroness's great sorrow every year when their festival of Passover approaches. You know of her terrible inner suffering because of her traitorous, rebellious daughter who stole from her mother, her relatives, her homeland, and her God. She left them to their groans and went and married a contemptible Jew. This wanton daughter embittered her mother's tender, upright life and made her old before her time. You remember what she said to me afterwards:

'Dear Doctor,' the baroness said to me before she left the country, 'I must leave you, my servants and my faithful citizens. My miserable daughter has expelled me and I must leave my homeland. I cannot stay with her any longer. In the beginning I had some hope that she would mend her ways and leave that wretched Jew. But now that she has borne him a son, there is no turning back. My daughter gave birth to a son whose father is a Jew! Dear doctor,' the baroness continued, her eyes filled with tears, 'I cannot bear this tragedy: I must leave the country. While this cursed pair, my daughter and her Jew, and their son are still there, I cannot return home. It's better that I should remain a restless wanderer on the earth[3] than that I should continually see this breach in my family with my own eyes. Doctor,' she added, 'could you please act on my behalf? Could you be of assistance to me?'

"These were the baroness's last words to me before she departed. I promised to come to her aid and kept my word. The dogs have long since devoured

---

3   Genesis 4:14.

that miserable Jew and the traitorous wife has already been judged by our Father in heaven—may God forgive her error. That miserable bastard son is now in my care. But why should I say anything more? I have prepared a gift for the baroness that will surely give her pleasure. Why should I reveal everything to you?! You'll see—and you'll know. No Christian in the world has ever received such a gift! And you, my brothers and sisters—you—when you understand, you'll certainly agree with me!"

2. Old Piotr Ilyich, Ruler of the Spirit World

Whether people understand the doctor or not, the liquor fermenting in their brains is not conducive to wisdom or mental acuity. But, no matter what, they agree with the doctor's words. They will never disagree with anything that the eminent Dr. Domshivski has to say.

Many who understand nod their heads with surprise and a kind of incredulity, and leave the important meeting. But the few who remain neither evade nor rebel. Their palates and throats are not thick with vodka. They are still sober, but their minds are unable to grasp the hints that the eminent doctor has given them. What thinking human being could understand such things? Apart from that, they're getting on in years, and many are relatives and friends of the estate's old butler, Piotr Ilyich. He is a strange, dim-witted old man. Despite being born and educated and having grown old on the von Schinken family estate, he acts like a stranger in their midst. The baroness loves old Piotr Ilyich, not only for his loyalty to her and her family, and the fact that this old eighty-eight-year-old man rocked her cradle and knows all the family's hidden secrets and errors. The baroness loves him for yet another reason: he rules over spirits and demons. He is a "pure sorcerer," as they introduce him here; he is the only one who knows how to subdue the impure demons who attack the estate and its mistress the Baroness von Schinken from time to time. These spirits have almost become evil members of the von Schinken family—cursed family members, who settled within the shadows of its confines hundreds of years ago and burst out of their mysterious dark hiding places from time to time, to assassinate the soul of the gentle baroness. These spirits are the domain of the entire family. Some appear to the baroness in her dreams and threaten her while she is reading on her Turkish sofa by the light of the full moon. They even drive her crazy at her most intimate moments, when the beauteous baroness is writhing in orgasmic convulsions with one of the lovers privileged to share her marvelous beauty and special grace. It has happened several times that, at the delicate, modest moment when she is passionately smothering one of her lovers with burning kisses all over his body, she finds herself bound with him to a green snake, that has slithered through the closed window from the thick outside primeval garden surrounding her palace, so full of different snakes and scorpions that it's impossible to keep them out. The green snake entwines the two living souls so tightly that it almost squeezes the life out of them, while its two wide-open red eyes fix their beams onto the lovers and its flickering black tongue licks its lips. At terrible hours such as these, the wretched baroness's bloodcurdling screams make one's hair stand on end. Piotr Ilyich comes at once, to rescue her. He alone can hear these spirits: no other human being dares to enter her portals at such an hour of corrupting, unclean spirits.

Piotr Ilyich doesn't use any type of force against these spirits and demons. He rules over them with the *goodness of his spirit,* with restrained, soft words, so different from all others in their sound and flavor. It is as if he caresses, embraces them with a kind of strange, excessive, and unique love. By these means he saves the tender baroness from the clutches of these accursed devils that lie in wait for her and abuse her at every turn.

This is the real cause of the baroness's love for this strange, grand old man.

But there are some spirits over which even Piotr Ilyich has no control. Even his soft words cannot placate and subdue them when they attack the baroness. When such spirits force her into their realm, Piotr Ilyich doesn't even try to appease them. He stands from afar and observes the baroness wallowing in distress like a fly fallen into the clutches of a spider, piercing it with its pincers and mercilessly sucking its blood out. When this happens the old man stands calmly and silently like a statue, without moving a muscle.

The baroness and her friend Dr. Domshivski call these spirits *the Jews.* They always appear after the baroness has had something to do with the village Jews.

Something of the kind happened to the baroness eight years ago: a small, insignificant occurrence related to the Jew Pesach Goldheimer's daughter. It was quite strange. The daughter had brought a pair of hard-to-find earrings set with two black precious stones from a faraway seaside city When the baroness saw them she coveted them with every fiber of her being: it was like a disease with her. A few days later, Pesach Goldheimer's daughter fell ill and the good Dr. Domshivski took her treatment upon himself. The day before she died, after the good doctor had spent an hour alone with her, the daughter made a will in which she requested to be buried together with her earrings. Three or four days after the burial the earrings turned up, displayed proudly on the baroness's little ears. A week after that, the baroness's ears swelled like dough kneaded with blood. It became impossible to remove the earrings because the doughy flesh covered their clasps and they had to be broken to save her ears. Because the baroness was afraid of wearing any other jewelry on her ears, the earrings were melted down and made into a fine inlaid ring, which almost cost her her life. She had worn the ring on her little finger for less than a day, when the finger softened into bloody dough as well and terrible pain almost drove her out of her mind. No one around had ever seen anything like it before. Even the doctor, with his vast experience—supposedly even with the supernatural world—and cold, hard, scientific logic, stood astonished. The baroness lay on her bed of pain, her aching hand hanging limply on the bed and the doughy, blood-soaked ringed finger stuck, through the darning of the thick Persian carpet, into the alder wood floor. The hole looked as if it had been made by an eagle's talon and no strength on earth could extract the finger from it. The baroness lay there at death's door, screaming incoherently:

"Piotr Ilyich! Piotr Ilyich! My dear grandfather! Go down to her!—Ask her!—Ask her to rise from her grave in the Jewish cemetery and visit me underneath the house—Ask her!—Ask her!—The doctor is guilty, not I!!—Take the accursed ring back down to her!—Dear Piotr Ilyich! Only you can do this!—Woe is me!—She is pulling me down!"

Piotr Ilyich stood as if astonished, lowered his face to the ground and mumbled, apparently to himself: "There are some demons against which no man on earth can stand—they are the demons born in ourselves, our own blood and brain—They are the fruit of our own souls—they don't listen to us—they demand sacrifice after sacrifice—"

Dr. Domshivski admitted tremblingly that the baroness had pleaded with him to steal the earrings from the grave. He had acceded to her request and cut off the ears together with the earrings. Piotr Ilyich advised that, for the baroness to return to health, her little finger with the ring be cut off. And so it was.

For the above reason, and many like it, the baroness loves the old man. Time after time he has straightened out her twisted soul.

But the people don't listen to the foolish man's sage advice. Their hearts are swollen with a sense of victory over the Jews, and the strong drink boils, ferments, and bubbles up from stomach to brain. When the burning sun with its dreadful secrets begins to set on the bloodred horizon, the awful evening with its terrible secrets begins. The estate servants start to set the festive table in honor of their dear Baroness von Schinken. To their horror, they find a Jewish baby in one of the concealed palace rooms, hands and feet bound, breathing out its tender soul in a dry, racking, suffering death rattle that is swallowed up into the black carpets.

3. The *Hillula* in Death's Courtyard[4]

But the baroness doesn't arrive and the wonderful celebrations are somewhat spoiled.

Her faithful retainers aren't in the least upset about this. The odor and taste of the fatty foods and strong drink don't lose their attraction in her absence: only Dr. Domshivski looks angry. "This is really unpleasant," he says. "Only yesterday she sent me a telegram asking me to prepare everything and telling me that she would definitely arrive in the evening. But she's still not here. Apart from the fact that it's costing a great deal of money, how can we complete this unique *hillula* without her, without our dearly beloved baroness?"

It's already the third day and the noisy banquet gets louder and louder as barrels of strong drink are emptied and endless wagons laden to the point of collapse arrive. But she is still not there! There are two entire tables, each fourteen hundred centimeters long, laden with bowls and plates filled with all sorts of savory dishes exuding pleasant pollution and the stench of boiled blood. For the past three days, jars, saucers, glasses, endlessly spill out their perfumed nectar like water. For the past three days, citizens and farmers have arrived from neighboring villages, to take the place of those who have left, falling down drunk. Drinking has reached excessive levels, hearts have become wild, healthy taut nerves loosened and torn like threadbare blankets, and upright, honest brains uncontrolled. The villagers wander under a bloodred sky amongst the darkness of open graves. They dance and sing amongst the rotting skeletons of dead Jews. They drink and drink, lying on the ground like joyful corpses, drinking without even tasting what they are drinking. They drink and

---

4   A *Yom Hillula* is another word for *yahrzeit* (the anniversary of a death) of a great *zaddik* (righteous teacher). Unlike a regular yahrzeit, which is marked with sadness and even fasting, a Yom Hillula is commemorated specifically through joy and festive celebration. Hameiri is being bitingly sarcastic.

moan, drink and sing voicelessly, drink and vomit, drink and vomit, over the open graves. The faithful villagers lie amongst the open graves and spill their guts up over the corpses.

This entire *hillula*—food, festivities, boozing—everything—takes place *in the Jewish cemetery.*

It's the honored doctor's miraculous invention—unequalled in village history—to move the celebration to the Jewish cemetery—how delightful! The doctor comes up with the idea the day before when, returning from the railway station without the baroness, he fears that the villagers' drinking might diminish. He stands on the upper palace balcony and, with a face flushed with excitement and wine, suggests that the feast be moved to a more interesting and important location—the courtyard of the Jewish cemetery. Jews who have been condemned to death but are still alive have, on his orders, collected the corpses in the street into one large cemetery pile. For the moment, they are locked up in the cemetery tent, awaiting their end. This is the first time that Dr. Domshivski has seen the natural beauty of a Jewish cemetery, whose location the Jews have taken captive. Look how the accursed Jews have snatched away the most beautiful location in the whole area—and for their dead! The cemetery is even lovelier than the estate's palace, with its beautiful garden, which serves as a summer house for Baroness von Schinken. How is it that no one has noticed this before?! Why did no one delay its theft?! That accursed Jew-loving whore, that intractable baroness's daughter, is to blame! She granted the lovely square to the accursed Jews to bury their dead! Those accursed Jews drove her crazy and cheated her into agreeing, thereby giving them a piece of land on which the most beautiful monastery in the country could have been built. And now she herself lies inside this Jewish cemetery. What a traitorous bitch!!

The suitability of this spot for such a celebration is self-evident.

"See for yourselves, dear brothers and sisters," says the good doctor with sacred envy, "how fortune smiles on the Jews even after they are dead. There, in the estate courtyard, trees are still bare and dry. But here, spring has arrived in all its glory. The trees are blossoming, the flowers emit their fragrance, and birdsong is heard between the fresh dahlias. When I saw all this, an excellent idea flashed into my mind. I ordered some of the imprisoned condemned Jews to move the laden tables to the cemetery. Brothers and sisters, you will surely agree with this decision and it goes without saying that the baroness will be happy with it as well."

The villagers are so sozzled that they would agree to anything. Hardly has the good doctor finished speaking, when a band of Jews arrives surrounded by armed guards. After a few moments, a wagon heavily laden with all sorts of good things arrives, pulled by an entire row of old Jews with unkempt beards and pale and wrinkled women, their children bound behind them. Swollen with hard labor, deaf, dumb, all feeling beaten out of them, they stagger towards the cemetery with their last strength.

The joyful crowd stands around, enjoying the wonderful spectacle. The village elders, sweating booze from every pore, stand with self-satisfied smirks on their twisted faces. The disheveled women chatter happily:

"Look! Look! They're getting exactly what they deserve!"

Only one old man stands to the side, lowers his head to the ground, and complains softly, as if prophesying a coming evil event: "There are some demons against which no man on earth can stand."

He leaves, disappearing inside one of the beautiful estate's hidden rooms.

It's as if the Jewish cemetery puts on a magical cloak. This orchard of sorrow suddenly opens up, revealing its hidden treasures, to sweeten their terrible celebration. The trees blossom before their time, slumbering flowers overflow with fragrance, enough to make a man drunk, and birds create a night-without-sleep,[5] overflowing with melancholy, tender song.

But, suddenly, a quiet moaning cleaves through this joyful-melancholy symphony of sounds mixed with debauched, drunken moans. The terrible sound saws the brain almost in half, evaporates the wine and strong drink, makes the hair stand on end, and strikes terror into the heart.

It's the groaning of the wretched condemned men, women, and children imprisoned in the cemetery "tent" awaiting a gruesome death. When the hoarse, half-crazed cries reach the ears of the celebrating crowd, they suddenly fall silent. They are seized with horror and the wine begins to evaporate.

One of the farmers asks:

"What is this, brother?"

"It's the voice of the Jews imprisoned in the tent until the baroness arrives. They have gone out of their minds."

The respected doctor doesn't allow them to sober up. He gives orders for the bonfire to be started immediately. While the good brothers and sisters go diligently about their work, a little klezmer group arrives, controlled by an

---

5   Exodus 12:42.

officer-conductor wielding a whip. The small, wretched, worm-like creatures, convulsed with suffering and fear, stand and play, moan and play, play and moan, while their backs and shoulders are being mercilessly whipped. Afterwards, to stop the whipping, the Jews begin to ask for requests and blow their trumpets with their last remaining strength. Sweat pours off them, the playing grows louder, drowning out the voices coming from the tent. The brothers under the tables between the disorderly, desecrated graves begin to sing.

"Play 'La Marseillaise!'" The conductor yells: "Play 'La Marseillaise!'"

He loves that tune. Some time ago, when he conducted the band on behalf of the "Jewish government," he ordered them to play the sacred melody, that hymn of national liberation. Now, he is ordering the band to play it again, this time under new orders, as a hymn to gruesome death.

He turns to the crowd:

"Brothers! You must help the players! You all know 'La Marseillaise'! That lovely Jewish melody! Anyone who can play an instrument, come forward!"

All the brothers can play an instrument and they certainly all know that Jewish tune. Many have sung it one occasion or another. They rise and yell "La Marseillaise" with open-mouthed drunken fury:

> We will plunder Jewish stores,
> Not one will remain,
> Rise up, rise up on the prey,
> From morning till evening!

The roars of both men and woman grow ever louder and more deafening, and the singing is carried on wings of the black night through the sleeping fields, startling the night owls and making them screech.

Suddenly—the noise of an approaching train.

The officer-conductor raises his eyes: he sees the illuminated carriage and commands:

"*Shh*! The illustrious baroness is coming!"

4. The Mark of Cain

A silent, respectful admiration fills the courtyard of death. Even the piercing light of lanterns on the tree branches trembles and the wind dies down for a moment. Those sitting around the table abandon their plates and cups, wipe their mouths, and rise in honor of the baroness. Those who have been singing raucously stand silent like wooden statues, eyes wide open fixed on the arriving great lady. It's as if an icy lightning bolt has struck the booze-soaked brains of those lying on the damp grass singing and cursing, suddenly shocking them sober and encouraging them to get up and look around.

But not one of them really expects to see her. After waiting for two and a half days, they have despaired of the baroness coming. She is, they think, not coming at all.

They have good reason to feel this way.

The baroness had no intention, up till now, of returning home.

The rumor was the fruit of Dr. Domshivski's fertile imagination: to prepare and encourage the people for his magnificent Festival of Decomposition. That is the reason for his charming lie: spreading the fiction that the baroness gave her permission for the celebration, he himself wrote the splendid telegram that made such a great impression on the dear villagers.

What about the burn on her face? Is the rumor that the baroness has sacrificed her beauty on the altar of the homeland real, or is it also a figment of Dr. Domshivski's sick mind?

The rumor?—Yes. The facts?—No.

The rumor that she saved the homeland, as put about by the eminent doctor, as well as the one about the Jewish woman's jealousy which the Jews perverted—both are products of his fertile imagination

But the fact itself *is a fact.*

When the baroness approaches the lit table and part of her face glows under her blue bonnet, *her dear brothers' eyes are transfixed by a bluish-red blemish glowing darkly from the face of their tender mistress by the lantern light. But the blemish is on her forehead, not her cheeks.*

If it wasn't for the blemish, the baroness wouldn't be returning home today. She really is coming! The scar is bringing her home. It isn't the fact that the doctor has sent one telegram after the other urging her to return and celebrate the splendid festival that he has prepared in her honor.

Let us go back in time: It's the blemish that has caused the baroness to suddenly change her itinerary and, instead of travelling to her wonderful island of Heligoland,[6] she is now sitting on a fast boat returning home *against her will.*

---

6   German island archipelago in the North Sea, part of Schleswig Holstein.

When the baroness receives the doctor's telegrams, she is on Jade Bay,[7] in the charming little town of Langwarden,[8] overlooking the blue North Sea. She has lived there for more than a year awaiting her homeland's liberation from Jewish oppression. She wanders in exile from town to town, waiting, waiting . . . But, in the meantime, she "puts aside her wanderer's staff," travelling around and enjoying the pleasures of the flesh. It's true that the dear homeland is in great danger, immersed in sorrow and grief. Every true patriotic heart is troubled by this. But at the end of the day a patriot's heart is made of flesh and blood, even in exile, and demands its due.

The baroness's heart demands a great deal from life, especially living as she does on the edge of Jade Bay, where the deep blue sea sings its love songs, constantly bringing powerful regiments, with their handsome commanders and generals, in from Southern climes on roaring waves.

The baroness's passionate heart demands seven times seven more from life than do others. A beautiful, sensuous, passionate woman, she is fixated not on the present or past but rather on the future. She is already forty and is trying with might and main to hold onto life with all its beauty. Her love interests center around the younger generation who, as if to anger her, cruelly maintain their dashing good looks despite all trouble and grief. Because Baroness von Schinken's fabled beauty is fading and gradually becoming a thing of the past.

The baroness is fully aware that her current flame will rapidly burn out and not be relit . . .

She is therefore insatiable.

The recent war has been her ally.

That same war that has shaken up the baroness's life like a boiling sea and given rise to new loves, new heroes, new storms—enough to lead to nervous exhaustion, almost madness.

Yes, her ally. However, the lovely bay has become less attractive to the baroness in one aspect. That same young generation of victorious young men whom the baroness pursues are now harbingers of doom—they darken her life and steal her rest.

Quite obviously, the young beauties who have competed for their affections and embittered her life are all Jewesses. What beautiful victor is not a Jewess in the eyes of the vanquished?

---

7   Jadebusen (Jade Bight), a bay on the North Sea coast of Germany.

8   Town on the Peninsula of Butjadingen, Lower Saxony, on the North Sea.

Things come to such a pass that the baroness decides to leave the beautiful bay, as full of young Jewesses as a swarm of wasps, and settle for a while on Heligoland Island, which is still Judenrein.

Recovering her full senses, she makes the final decision.

She sits in the boat departing for the island archipelago.

Her new confidante, who has not yet been her guest, accompanies her on the trip. Her name is Fräulein Shabata de Barbanel. Fräulein de Barbanel is a Spaniard, born of a noble family who have come down in the world. Within a short time, she and the baroness become bosom companions. The baroness loves her for her refined personality, uniquely acute intellect, but more than anything for the fact that she has finally found someone who understands her. This understanding finds special expression in one of the baroness's principal viewpoints—virulent antisemitism. The baroness has never before experienced a relationship like the one with Fräulein de Barbanel: the young lady understands the baroness's hatred of the Jews, how she perceives the hidden danger they pose to all humanity! All this without the need for words, opinions, lengthy arguments, or other well-known methods of expression. Just silence and a unique smile. The baroness pours out her heart in righteousness wrath on Jewish chutzpah, the shamelessness of their women. On the other hand, her tender soul is enveloped in simple thoughts and mysterious but divine spirits. Fräulein de Barbanel says nothing in reply. Instead, a strange kind of smile hovers over her face; she looks straight at the baroness with her dark eyes, and says:

"Yes, yes, madame, this is a very old, leprous wound. The Jews—yes, the Jews. There are types of leprous maladies in the world that no doctor can heal."

These words remind the baroness of what her beloved old Piotr Ilyich often used to say about evil demons. After all, he shares her hatred of the Jews and feels their malignant presence in the depths of his soul.

Now, when the baroness has decided to sail to pure, Jew-free Heligoland, where she can find some peace from her stormy life, Fräulein de Barbanel smiles and says, in her usual quiet way:

"Yes, yes, madame. There are types of leprous maladies in the world that no doctor can heal. But, for all that, return, return. Everything will be wonderful over there."

They sit together on the boat.

At midnight the boat is still at anchor. Before the baroness arranges her things prior to going to sleep, she picks up Dr. Domshivski's frequent telegrams calling her back home for some great celebration or other. She re-reads them, throws them down, and exclaims:

"Ay! I'll still have time to travel home and sniff the odor of roast pork! The war is not finished yet!"

The baroness lies down on her soft bed, sends her young friend away, closes the door of her cabin, crosses herself piously three times in Orthodox fashion, and goes to sleep.

But hardly has she fallen asleep properly when the boat weighs anchor and begins to move. The baroness is startled for a moment, then closes her eyes again. But she cannot fall asleep. As soon as the boat moves, a child in an adjacent cabin panics and begins to cry.

The baroness tries to close her shell-like ears, but to no avail. The impudent child keeps on screaming. The faster the boat moves, the louder the child screams.

The baroness gets up and calls the cabin attendant.

"Please," she says, "try to do something about this. People are trying to sleep but the child keeps screaming."

The attendant promises to do something about it and leaves.

The baroness covers her head with the blanket, but it doesn't help. She can't fall asleep. That accursed child just keeps on crying. It becomes a real screaming fit.

"This is ridiculous" she says. "On a splendid, luxurious ship like this—a child screaming? Enough already!" She rings for the cabin attendant again.

"Mon dieu," she says to the attendant, "this is ridiculous! Tell the parents to control their child! This is no time for it to scream!"

"But there is no child there, madame," the attendant says, "I have looked and there is no one there."

She leaves.

"No child?" the baroness mumbles. "This attendant is really abusing me. No child, when the screaming fit doesn't stop? Mon dieu! It's impossible to sleep!"

Yes, she can't sleep. The crying gets louder and louder, penetrating her ear drums. The baroness rolls around on the bed.

Willingly or unwillingly, she begins to listen to the voice of the crying child, which stops for a moment of two, then starts again. When the baroness listens carefully, she can distinguish two things. Firstly, it's the voice of a boy not a girl. Secondly, it's not a cry of obstinacy, but *one of pain*. This is a cry of inner distress, physical pain, that doesn't stop. A cry of torment.

Apart from the crying there is no sound of mother or father, no calming, quieting voice. The crying becomes more penetrating: a cry of suffering, complaint, begging for compassion, moaning.

A moan that resembles a death rattle.

A strange and terrible thing.

Who is abusing this little boy?

The baroness's anger turns to pity.

She is overwhelmed with compassion for the suffering boy who is crying and begging for help. It's impossible to simply lie and listen to this. Who would torture a little boy without let or hindrance?

She gets up, puts on the light, and leaves her cabin. She wakes up Fräulein de Barbanel and tells her about it. They both listen.

Silence.

"It's a hallucination, madame," says Fräulein de Barbanel. "Such hallucinations do occur. I've seen them before. You're a little tired and angry, madame."

"That is possible," the baroness says doubtfully. "Let's go into the adjoining cabin to see if it's true. After all, I heard the crying with my own ears."

The young woman agrees. She knocks on the door of the adjacent cabin, excuses herself, and asks if there is a crying child there.

They are amazed to see an old Jew in the cabin.

"A little boy crying? Here?" the old man asks with a smile. "Not only are all my sons married, but they even have their own sons—my grandsons, may God preserve them in health and life. I, madame, I have long since left the realm of children!"

He laughs.

The young woman goes to the baroness to calm her down.

'Some old Jew or other is sitting in the cabin," she says smilingly.

The baroness's face twists in terror.

"Mon dieu," she says almost in tears, "Jews, even here! I cannot escape from them!"

The young woman smiles her unique smile.

"Yes, madame. They are here, there, everywhere."

She concludes, in her own tender way:

"There are leprous maladies in the world that no doctor can heal."

She excuses herself pleasantly and politely, and leaves the cabin.

After a few moments, the continued crying starts to drive the baroness out of her mind. She gets up in fury and makes a terrible fuss throughout the boat. The captain must at long last restore order! In the meanwhile, a thought flashes into her mind: an old Jew, in that cabin? Is it possible that the Jew is jewifying there? It's spring—their festival of Passover—either now, or in the near future. No question about it! Jews do terrible things during this time! Everybody knows how they bake their matzoth with the blood of children!

She calls one of the crew and orders him to investigate the cabin immediately. How annoying! Terrible! Just think, an old Jew there! Yes! On this boat!

The sailor quietens her down. That's an improbable, stupid story, quite unsuitable for a gracious lady like herself. But yes, to calm her down, he will investigate.

He speaks to the old Jew, excuses himself a thousand times, and leaves.

The baroness, angry in body and soul, lies down and listens carefully. It seems to her that the boy's crying has become a real death rattle.

Even she starts to believe that the whole thing is a hallucination.

She closes her ears and tries to sleep, but the little boy doesn't stop crying. The crying is so tender, so weak and heartfelt, that she starts to melt inside. And now the child starts to form words: the words of a small child suffering terrible torment and begging for help:

"*Gra'mama! Gra'mama! Babushka! The ugly doctor! Gadkiy doktor! Gra'mama! Babushka dorogaya! Ya vas lyublyu!*"[9]

The baroness's heart starts to flutter and pound, almost strangling her. Her eyes bulge and are momentarily blinded. She opens her eyes wide and it's as if the furniture in the room is dancing. "God in Heaven! That voice! No! I must be ill! My young friend told me that I'm very tired! No! Impossible!"

She listens again very, very carefully. She feels her eyes: they are wet with tears. She tries to speak, but her throat is suffocating. "No! Impossible! I am ill!

"Miss Shabata! Miss de Barbanel!" She shrieks with terrible force and awful terror.

The young woman becomes alarmed. She embraces the baroness with her tender arms and calms her down.

"Dear madam! Beautiful, tender madam! Calm yourself! I'll call the doctor!"

---

9   Russian: Grandmother! Grandmother! Babushka! The ugly doctor! Dear Grandmother! I love you!

"No! No!" The baroness shakes her shock of unkempt hair. "No doctor! Stay and listen with me! Maybe the crying will stop. This is no hallucination!"

Fräulein de Barbanel sits on the bed and strokes the baroness's fevered brow.

The baroness lies, stares at the ceiling like a frozen, immovable statue. After that, her entire body begins to tremble. She grabs Fräulein de Barbanel's hand, raises her head, and says with bulging eyes:

"Do you hear? Do you hear?"

The young woman listens and listens, looks at the baroness, and says, with her usual pleasant smile through full, plump lips:

"Yes, madame, I hear a little boy is crying, begging for help," she emphasizes in a thin and serious voice, full of inflection. "'*Gra'mama!*' He's about two years old and is suffering. But the child is Jewish."

As soon as she hears this, Baroness von Schinken's empurpled, enraged face turns pale as death. She raises first her head, then her whole body, fixes her weak eyes on Fräulein de Barbanel and says in terror:

"*That is my grandson!*"

She collapses on the bed.

Then young woman understands immediately. To be completely sure, she embraces the baroness lying immobile on the bed with eyes closed, and asks:

"Is he a Jew?"

"Yes," the baroness mumbles, eyes closed. "Yes, dear fräulein, he's a Jew. I'm going out of my mind," she says slowly but with terrible emphasis." I'm going insane. Protect me, dearest Fräulein Shabata, save me! I want to live!"

"Go back home tomorrow morning!" Fräulein de Barbanel whispers in her ear and kisses her forehead. "Yes, you must go home: and, if you will permit, I will travel with you. Do you agree, madame?"

"Yes," the baroness stammers voicelessly, and adds:

"Please bring me some tea with Chartreuse, or perhaps a little absinthe."

The young woman lights the little stove and prepares the cups. In the meantime she leaves, entering her cabin for a moment. The baroness, left alone, opens her eyes and, hair unkempt, nerves stretched to the limit, and half naked, she rises, stands, and listens. It's as if her body is gripped with fear: she walks a few steps to the boiling stove and listens—listens. She nods her head as if sharing a terrible sorrow. Her face contorts and her eyes stream with large, heavy tears. She kneels, clasps her hands in prayer, raises them up, and says in weeping voice filled with tender entreaty:

"Mon infant! Mon cher infant! Ne pleure pas! Ne pleure pas! Weine nicht, mein teures Kindchen! Je viens á toi! Je viens![10] Dear grandson, I am hurrying back to you. Don't cry! I am coming to save you! I'll save you, mon cher enfant!

"Mon Dieu! Merciful God! Have pity on your sinful servant! Mon Dieu! Mon cher Dieu!"

She falls to the floor, weeping bitterly.

While falling she knocks the little stove over and the boiling water spills onto her face. If it wasn't for the fact that the Fräulein enters at that exact time, her face would have been consumed by fire.

The Fräulein calls for the ship's doctor. They pick the baroness up and put her to bed. He finds out that, by the grace of God, no great harm has been done, but she will have a scar on her forehead. The burn is serious, but it will heal.

The baroness lies unconscious for a short while without knowing what has happened. She is only awakened when the ship's whistle signals their arrival.

Half an hour later, the baroness and her confidante, Fräulein de Barbanel, are sitting in another boat returning to Wilhelmshaven, and from there on to the Black Sea.

So, the baroness returns home.

Against her will.

When she reaches her estate and Dr. Domshivski lovingly welcomes her, the baroness is tired, withdrawn, and angry. The first words she hurls at him are:

"Where's the boy?"

The good doctor freezes, horrified. He can't understand why she should ask such a thing, nor can he find the words to respond. But he keeps his cool and extricates himself from the confusion by lying:

"The boy died a while ago."

The baroness breathes heavily, as if freed from a terrible burden, and says:

"Thank God. Please introduce yourselves."

Dr. Domshivski and Fräulein de Barbanel get acquainted.

After a few moments, their conversation turns to important estate matters of interest to the baroness.

---

10 Mixture of French and German: Don't cry, my dear child. I'm coming to you. I'm coming.

When the servants arrive to welcome her, the baroness's face brightens up a little and her eyes begin to sparkle as in the old days. When the loyal servants see the burn on her forehead, they are reminded of the doctor's words and their bodies tremble with a sacred shiver at the sight of their exalted mistress.

What a holy soul she is!

They kiss her tender hands, as if sanctified by her presence.

Only the doctor himself stands astonished and doesn't understand what is going on.

How could this be? He himself had fabricated that story. Impossible! The news about the burn reached him two days ago. Who told him? Some officer or other had given him the news. And he didn't believe it then! Amazing!

When he examines the burn carefully, a pleasant shiver runs down his spine. At that exact moment, he believes in his heart that the burn is holy. He approaches the baroness, bows down to her, and says:

"Dear, exalted madame, allow me to kiss your holy brow." He kisses her forehead.

At that moment, Dr. Domshivski feels that he too is an extraordinary personage. This burn is a miracle of miracles!

He addresses the baroness again, with a feeling of shared sanctity:

"My dear baroness, this scar adds to your grace."

He kisses her burn again.

"Where is my dear old Piotr Ilyich?" asks the baroness.

But no one knows where he is. The servants say that it's already been three days since he disappeared from the estate and no one has seen him since.

Upon hearing this, Fräulein de Barbanel responds:

"A really old man with bushy eyebrows? Yes, I saw him a minute ago," she says with her customary serious smile." I saw him stand here, madame. He looked at you for a moment, crossed himself, and quietly stammered something into his long beard. I could only make out a few words. 'The mark of Cain,' he mumbled in a soft whisper. 'The mark of Cain.' Then he disappeared. I wouldn't have noticed him, if not for his long beard."

"A strange old man," the baroness replies, deep in thought. "I love him and you will love him too, fräulein, when you get to know him."

"*I have loved him for a long time,*" Fräulein de Barbanel replies with a strange smile and she sits down to tea with the baroness.

After a while, the "beautiful people" of Schinkanovka come to welcome the baroness and to invite her to the splendid festivities which they have in her honor. On with the drama!

5. The Last Supper

Baroness von Schinken's wild nature lurches between two stormy extremes: reckless love affairs on one hand and her daughter's offspring on the other. Fear of angels of destruction doesn't require much time or exceptional means to swing from one madness to the other. There are natures whose lives are one long series of lurching, which don't occur by accident but are part and parcel of their lives. These horrors are the oxygen of their souls and fear of them is a kind of supreme spice which makes boredom a soothing, therapeutic refuge.

Baroness von Schinken is such a stormy soul. Clearly, the new-old surroundings to which she has returned after her long separation have changed. The new face of her wretched country, because of the long and exhausting war, astonishes her and, within a few short hours, changes her spirit for the better, to what it was before. She feels healthy and whole, as if having awoken from a long, sweet sleep.

After dinner and several glasses of good red Rhenish wine have fertilized and rejuvenated her tired body, she immediately agrees to Dr. Domshivski's invitation to join the celebration.

The good doctor fills her in on recent events. It doesn't take much to stir up her ire against the hated enemy who has laid waste to her beloved homeland and turned her into a wretched outcast, a restless wanderer on the earth. She at once feels that all her time living outside the country has been one long series of suffering and exile, without estate, home, or the accessories of life. Dr. Domshivski doesn't need to say much. It's enough for him to remind her of the Jews' evil acts: how they have captured her pure and beautiful palatial home, defiled the holy icons, abused her sacred liturgical objects and the appurtenances of her home—her horses, carriages, servants, clothes, even the clothes of her late husband Baron Valerius von Schinken (may he rest in paradise). On top of all this—merciful God! How they have defiled her sacred, canopied bed by screwing their miserable, contemptible women in it! These stories are enough to make her delicate blue blood boil and forget her difficult journey, all the countries outside her beloved homeland, and all the world's misfortune together. Baroness von Schinken sees it as her sacred duty to return to the old ways and perform great deeds which stir up body and soul for exceptional events.

And of course to participate in the Festival of Jewish Decomposition!

The good doctor whispers the charming secret into her ear: the dear brothers and sisters have prepared a wonderful, unique gift for their beloved mistress who has suffered so much on their behalf, worried about them unceasingly, and sacrificed her life on the altar of their redemption.

He whispers the secret to her, but not the nature of the gift. After all, a proper gift must be a surprise!

The baroness goes unhesitatingly to the celebration. She even forgets to ask where it will be held.

She sits comfortably in an illuminated carriage with Dr. Domshivski and Fräulein de Barbanel—and off they go.

It's a moonlit night and the baroness is feeling good. But the reason for this pleasant feeling isn't clear. Is it because of her new surroundings or the expectation of her dear servants awaiting her at the celebration?

The carriage in which she is travelling with the doctor is closed on all sides and the road leads directly towards the moon. Not a single beam of light penetrates through the windowpanes. Immersed in their own thoughts, they sit silently side by side. The baroness shakes herself awake when the train begins to move and moonbeams penetrate through the windows, as if a kind of thrill suddenly courses through her body. She asks:

"Where is this celebration going to take place?"

The doctor smiles through his black moustache, winks at her cunningly but graciously, and says:

"In the Jewish cemetery."

What a pleasant surprise! The baroness opens her eyes wide, revealing a face filled with satisfied surprise.

"The Jewish cemetery?" she asks in wonder mixed with fright and vague enjoyment. "The Jewish cemetery?" Fright competes with enjoyment. "The Jewish cemetery?"

"Yes," Dr. Domshivski smiles.

This smile shakes off the baroness' indecision and she decides that this is indeed a very good thing. She smiles back and says:

"Nu, doctor, you are a talented man. A true genius! In their cemetery? All right, dear doctor, all right. Fantastic!" "Nu, Fräulein de Barbanel, what do you think? Do you like the good doctor?"

Fräulein de Barbanel, who knows exactly what is going on and where, smiles in satisfaction, looks straight into Dr. Domshivski's eyes, and says quietly with a pleasant little laugh:

"Yes, honored doctor, you are a well-known genius. But in the same way, you are a dangerous man. Every genius is dangerous to some degree. Genius is a tragic thing. But remember what the wise king said: 'Pride goes before destruction.' You know how wise King Solomon was."[11]

And she smiles, showing once more her warm, lively nature.

Dr. Domshivski feels as if he has been elevated. He appreciates the compliments that have been paid him and laughs with proud self-satisfaction:

"He-he-he! You are absolutely correct!"

The baroness overflows with pleasure.

"Fräulein de Barbanel's esprit is typical of a pure-bred Spaniard" she says seriously. "Only Spaniards are gifted with such penetrating intellects. In this respect they are even superior to the French!"

The fräulein concludes with a request for forgiveness:

"Perhaps superior even to the wise king!" she says, laughing loudly.

The baroness is a little surprised by this laugh. This is the first time that she has heard her dear companion laughing so loudly. It's a pleasant and interesting laugh, but also a little strange. Why has this laugh made such an impression on her?

The strange laugh sends a shiver down the baroness's spine. Without knowing why,[12] she jumps up, looks out of the carriage window, sees that they are going the wrong way, and says in panic:

"Wait! Wait! Stop! Where are we going? This is not the way! Wait! Go back! Back! This is not the way! We're lost!"

Dr. Domshivski panics as well. He gets up, opens the carriage door, and looks. After that he calms down somewhat, and says quietly:

"No. Madame. I'm sure that we are on the right road! I know the way there very well! Even the train knows! By my life, I am positive that I won't lead you astray! This road leads straight to the cemetery!"

Fräulein de Barbanel who has been sitting quietly the whole time throughout the baroness's panic, smiles and adds:

"Not only this, but all roads lead to the cemetery."

---

11   Proverbs 16:18: "Pride goes before destruction, and a haughty spirit before a fall."

12   Hameiri uses both Hebrew words for why: *madua* (past) and *lama* (future).

The baroness feels a chill in her soul. She sits looking at the glowing moon, rubs her hands together, and says:

"I feel cold. Spring has arrived, but I feel cold."

"Don't worry, my dear baroness," says Dr. Domshivski, "The celebration that we have prepared will not only warm your body, but scorch your soul as well. Ha-ha-ha!"

Fräulein de Barbanel smiles in agreement. And so they travel onward. The carriage window is open and the pale reddish moon, which at the last moment has changed its color from silver to pure gold, drifts between thick, heavy clouds which obstruct its path. Yet the moon prevails, passes them, and continues onwards on its appointed route. However, the destination is not purposed there, nor in the sky, but here, where it shines continuously. The moon beams straight into the carriage, as if leading it on its way. It finally pushes the clouds aside and drifts onward, ever onward with the carriage which, slowly then more rapidly, approaches its destination.

The baroness feels all of this while she is looking straight at the moon. It's as if the cold, hard rays of this strange planet have pierced the carriage and are pulling it along like molten prongs, leading it onwards, onwards to its final destination. She neither sees nor knows where they are going, but feels that something strange and terrible awaits her there, something that plays on her nerves, makes her hair stand on end, something that is not in her power to remove. But she cannot move from her place, let alone evade the beams of the cruel moon. She *doesn't want to evade* this terrible thing which, apart from making her hair stand on end, is also pleasurable, stimulating her nerves to the point of intoxication. The gentle breeze carries on its wings sounds, or fragments of sounds, louder and weaker at the same time, weak and strong voices intermittently. Suddenly the train slows down it's pace, jerking the passengers with it. They have arrived at the noisy Jewish cemetery.

When the baroness gets out of the carriage, a fantastic, delusory picture appears before her eyes and alcohol-soaked mind. A picture that no "free theater" anywhere in the world has presented before her in her travels afar.

She sees a large, fresh garden full of very old and young trees entangled with one another. Between their tendrils gleam small intertwined green and gray snakes. Flowers, scattered all over the garden without any order, exude an astonishingly heavy odor which arouses first the nose and lungs then the heart and brain, seeping into the blood like a warm, sweet, intoxicating flood. The garden is surrounded by a wall, and multicolored lanterns large and small spread their trembling light. Over them, the full moon shines through the black clouds with its pure light, illuminating the colors and their wandering shadows into a pleasant dreamy picture which casts waves of ether in the blood and arouses in the released soul a desire beyond the life and thoughts of . . .

The baroness doesn't properly understand the thoughts swirling around in her head. Only now does she begin to feel a little tired.

She stands next to the carriage for a moment, as if busy with her clothes. In the meanwhile, she gives herself over to the image before her and the swirling noise—together, they renew her soul.

The garden—that is to say, the cemetery—with its trees, flowers, and crooked monuments shining whitely with their black engravings, standing in wondrous silence, has a depressing effect on her. It's as if all this has made her nervous and astonished. But the ebullient crowd; long tables laden with food and drink; drunk farmers sitting, lying vomiting between the open graves; this entire night of vigil[13]—the hellish cacophony of moans, curses, songs, screams, music—all these at first confuse her completely, but then have a completely opposite effect. They change her back to the old Baroness von Schinken who parties at the seaside and in tumultuous towns looking for sensuous pleasures, but always returning to her estate, to her serfs and loyal servants, who give her something that is missing in those foreign lands, something which satisfies her hungry soul.

She descends from the train and the deafening noise stops at the moment of her arrival. When she sees the drunk and half-drunk farmers rising from their places, leaving their overflowing dishes and cups, wiping their food-stuffed lips in her honor, bowing low, and crossing themselves piously three times, the baroness feels a pleasant thrill of sanctity running down her spine—something that she has never felt before. The feeling turns at once into soft and tender love. When she approaches and asks after their welfare, she acts as if she wants to embrace them all in one sweeping movement.

At that moment Baroness von Schinken really loves her dear, faithful serfs and servants who have raised her to sainthood. Of course, she is used to their

---

13   Hameiri is being sarcastic. The All-Night Vigil is a service of the Eastern Orthodox Church (and Eastern Catholic Church) consisting of an aggregation of the three canonical hours of Vespers, Matins, and the First Hour. The vigil is celebrated on the eves of Sundays and of major liturgical feasts. It could also refer to Passover eve (Exodus 12:42).

respect and honor. But what are all the compliments in the world compared to sanctification? They actually cross themselves before her!

This wild and lustful soul actually feels her face radiating the sanctity of the Holy Virgin. Her tender visage is actually surrounded by rays of glory, a kind of heavenly light. Which gracious lady in Wilhelmshaven or Paris has ever had a similar experience?

Filled with feelings of victory, the baroness cannot restrain herself. She bows to her confidante Fräulein de Barbanel, and whispers in her ear with unrestrained joy:

"Well, dear signora, there is still a corner of the great world in which I am loved with absolute purity. No insolent Jewish bitch in the world can ever aspire to such love!"

The baroness intuits that the Fräulein will respond angrily and doesn't let her speak. Instead, she turns to the crowd around her and, with a mischievous manner and happy, joyful demeanor, says, accompanying her words with hand gestures:

"Nu, dear brothers and sisters, don't interrupt your celebration on my behalf! Enjoy, sing, play, drink, get drunk! The hour has come when we'll finally be free of the accursed Jews!"

A tumult of "Hurrah" cuts through the chilly air. The baroness, Dr. Domshivski, and the Fräulein sit down at table, the music begins to thunder and hoarse, drunken, grating voices rise up to heaven on the wings of the moonlit night.

An entire hour passes in debauchery, boozing, moaning, yelling, breaking of dishes, and wild laughter. The eyes of the crowd wander aimlessly, hearts are swollen with wine, and brains wild and uncontrolled. Dr. Domshivski rises, grabs onto the table so as not to fall back into his chair, and starts to speak in honor of the illustrious baroness and the sacred celebration.

Wonderful and unique is the honored doctor's speech. It's true that strong drink has driven him a little mad. But he gets hold of himself, fights against his drunkenness, and speaks in a loud voice, with careful moderation and jerky speech that fails at times but still explains what he has to say.

He begins by saying that this celebration is not coincidental. Today is the memorial day for one of the most splendid revenge pogroms carried out by one of the people's greatest heroes hundreds of years ago. He knows the history of the Jews only too well—no rabbi knows it better. Everyone knows that it is a burden imposed on him. But the dear brothers and sisters don't know exactly who stands before them. He, Dr. Domshivski himself, is a direct descendant of one of the most famous heroes of Slav chronicles. He is the grandson of the famous Cossack Gonta.[14] Based upon several written genealogical documents in his possession, he is the Chosen One of history! History itself has chosen him to pass judgment over this cruel nation, which has abused pious Christians for thousands upon thousands of years without let or hindrance. The doctor explains to them the privilege of belonging to this generation and the value of their holy war against the Jews. Their entire raison d'être is to take revenge on the cursed Jews. The respected doctor also explains the religious significance of their holy feast.

"This feast," he says "is the Last Supper. Yes, brothers and sisters—the Last Supper. You surely know about Christ's Last Supper. Which faithful Christian doesn't know about Christ's Last Supper before He ascended to heaven? But I doubt that you know the secret reason behind it. Only a very few Chosen Ones in the Christian world know, in the same way that very few know exactly why the Son of God died in such pain and suffering before His ascension to heaven. Why did He die in such pain and suffering? He had to die in this way only because *He was born to a Jew*, dear brothers and sisters! Yes, dear brothers and sisters, it was not He who died, but the Jew in him! Yes, the Jew in Him died a gruesome death, but the Christian was resurrected to everlasting life! Therefore, dear brothers and sisters, at this hour when all the Jews die by our hands, the feast we are celebrating at their death is also a Last Supper. In order that our last supper is similar to Christ's Last Supper in all respects, *we have prepared its Jew to die a gruesome death.*

He indicates that they should look to the side.

Everyone turns their faces to the right, where the officer-conductor of the Jewish band brings in a tall Jew with a small beard and black curly hair, with hands tied behind him and wandering eyes. He says nothing. His swarthy face is pale, but completely calm. He is silent.

When the baroness looks at the young man, she is momentarily horrified and doesn't believe her eyes. He is a young shohet from the village next to

---

14   Ivan Gonta was one of the leaders of an uprising of Ukrainian Cossacks rebelling against the Polish-Lithuanian Commonwealth, who massacred the Jews of Uman in 1768. He was immortalized in the controversial epic by Ukraine national poet Taras Shevchenko (1814-1861) *Haidamaky.*

Schinkanovka, son-in-law of Pesach Goldheimer, husband of that accursed Jewess with the earrings.

Baroness von Schinken looks at him and all sorts of confused, unclear thoughts run amok in her drunken brain. But when she recognizes him, her confused thoughts crystallize into a feeling of overpowering revenge. Is not this the husband of that accursed woman who stole her tranquility and her little finger? The baroness turns to her Fräulein with wandering eyes, to explain who the Jew is to her, but her place is empty. She is not there.

Where has she gone?

The baroness is too drunk to worry about it. She isn't there—so what? She'll soon return. She is standing near the wall. No, she isn't. Is she smiling? No, she isn't smiling. How strange she looks when she smiles. But now she isn't there, she isn't smiling. The doctor knows how strange it is. What does he know? The dear doctor knows everything, doesn't he? What a wonderful discovery—the Jew in Christ! How strange—how charming—the honored doctor. He is speaking and Christ is silent. The doctor speaks and Christ sits at her side. Yes, she is the Virgin Mary. The Jew is Christ. He is silent. How absurd—how lovely—the doctor speaks—she understands.

"Yes," says the doctor. "This is the Last Supper—this Jew is the last Jew in the world. But before we cleanse ourselves of him and send him to meet his maker, he himself must partake of his own Last Supper."

So speaks the doctor. Yes, the doctor is wise. the wisest of the wise. It is all so splendid— but where is the Fräulein?—and the doctor speaks, he speaks to her, yes, he speaks to the baroness. Yes, she understands, she understands everything—a gift! Yes, a gift! Yes, yes, she remembers—a gift, a dear gift! Absurd! Splendid! A gift!

Baroness von Schinken's sozzled brain mixes up images, concepts, memories, and feelings attached to them. She feels that this is something new, strange, absurd, but deeply moving. She doesn't know whether she should laugh at it or not.

Suddenly she sees something that she doesn't understand at all. She does not understand, but she senses it is new. Yes, something new and somewhat peculiar. And a little bit absurd. Yes, absurd, but also touching, and she does not know if one can laugh at this or not . . .

She sees and does not see. Sees and cannot believe:

The officer goes out and returns, carrying a large golden platter *in his outstretched arms. On the platter, she clearly sees the body of a small two-year-old boy, his body covered with third-degree burns and blisters. The little body is almost roasted.*

The smell of burning meat wafts out of it.

The face of the dead boy is so burned as to be unrecognizable, but it certainly is a little boy, yes, a roasted boy—How strange—how absurd—she must laugh—yes, it's impossible not to laugh—Ha-ha-ha—yes!—and another thing; yes, yes, she can see it clearly: inside the chest, over there—yes—*a knife stuck in the child's chest—up to the haft—that is not laughable—but—strange—Ha-ha-ha!*

Do any of the drunk brothers and sisters see what the baroness sees? It's impossible to know. They are now so drunk that they look but see nothing.

But the baroness sees.

And Dr. Domshivski sees.

And the officer-conductor sees.

And the Jew who is bound hand and foot sees.

The baroness blinks her red, piggy eyes. She has no idea what she is looking at. She blinks them and has no idea why she is blinking.

The doctor takes the knife out of the little boy's chest and gives it to the silent shohet, sitting as if frozen, not even moving his eyelids.

The doctor takes up the word again.

The baroness listens and understands.

"This is your gift, esteemed madame! This is your gift. All of us—myself, the villagers, the estate servants—offer it to you!"

The blood in the baroness's veins begins to flow like coagulated, decomposing pus. She has no idea what is going on. She feels that something is happening, but her throat is blocked and doesn't allow her to say anything.

She wants to open her mouth, but a hoarse voice prevents her from doing so. The voice comes from far away, from the voices of many weeping women:

"Ah—ah—ah—ah! Gotenyu, schlechter! Au—Au—Bistikh Nokem! Ah—Au!"[15]

After the moaning comes wild laughter:

"He-He-He—Gotenyu, herziger! Bistikh Nokem! Nokem an deine Kinder? Ah-ah!"[16]

"Ha-ha-ha"

---

15   Garbled Yiddish: My God, evil people, you are vengeful!

16   Garbled Yiddish: My God, my dear! You are vengeful! Vengeance for your children?

The gang of men, women, and children imprisoned in the cemetery tent burst outside and approach the celebrants with tumult, confused screams, wailing, curses, and weeping. They surround the tables. One screams, another weeps, yet another laughs. A terrible laugh. Others tear the lanterns from the trees. Some fall on the graves, bellowing and weeping.

Suddenly—a shot!

The officer has shot one of them.

Chaos ensues. The celebrants scatter to the four winds. Only a few remain, snoring on the ground between the graves.

The baroness, shocked to the marrow of her bones, stammers:

"Stop! St-op in the name of God! Stop shooting them! Give me the revolver!"

She stands on her weak legs, wipes sweat from her face, takes the revolver, and puts it on the table.

Silence.

In the murky silence, by the light of a dim moon, a rustle comes from the black trees and the image of a woman appears from behind the cemetery east wall.

A young, deathly pale woman dressed in white approaches.

It's the baroness's dead daughter.

Baroness Magdalena von Schinken.

She approaches her mother.

She gets nearer and nearer. Yes, it is really her daughter. What was her name? Magdalena? No, Sarah Magdalena—yes, Sarah, her beautiful, delicate, beloved—*dead* daughter.

The mother stands with legs glued to the ground, rooted to the spot, and cannot move a muscle. She wants to approach her daughter, but cannot.

The red moon appears from behind the clouds in all its terrible brightness. And her only daughter gets closer and closer. She stands—bows respectfully and says—is she speaking? No, her lips are not moving. But nevertheless her mother hears words:

"Bienvenue, maman, welcome! My mother, my own dear mother!"

Does the doctor hear? The baroness is afraid to move and look at him. Is he here? Yes, he is here.

The daughter repeats:

"Bienvenue, maman, ma chère maman! How much I love you, my sweet mother!" The voice is so tender, so pleasant, so sweet.—

The baroness's legs are stuck to the ground.

Her hands are as heavy as stone.

Her daughter approaches her—to shout!—no—impossible—her daughter approaches—she is so beautiful—dead—awful!—approaches.

She stands before her and, without embracing her, bows her head and kisses her on the forehead.

"You are holy, my dear mother—you are the Virgin Mary."

The baroness hears but doesn't answer.

Cry?—she cannot.

How good it would be to cry!

And embrace her—the dead.

She wants so much to embrace her!

Her hands are outstretched—and her daughter has already left her—no—she approaches the dead boy on the table, raises the corpse with trembling hands, raises him to her mouth, and kisses him longingly in calm and silent sorrow.

She stands up straight again—the boy to her right side—it is her son—yes—the little grandson—little Chaim Shmuel—he is smiling through his disfigured face—his mother is smiling as well—standing and smiling with her son—their faces are bleak, bleak—yet they smile.

The baroness begins to choke.

She cannot remain silent anymore.

Her heart is dying of distress and love.

She summons up the final power in her mouth and throat and starts to speak with melancholy love and great compassion:

"Mon enfant! Mon cher enfant!"

Suddenly there is a wild laugh—her daughter turns her back on her—and laughter— who is laughing?!—Who is laughing at her?—Who dares laugh at her?! Oh—it's old Piotr Ilyich's hoarse laugh! He is laughing?!—Yes, he laughs—laughs and repeats his terrible stupidity:

"There are some demons—Ha-ha-ha!"

Who else is laughing?—Yes—oh—Fräulein de Barbanel!?

She is laughing as well, with her usual words:

"There are leprous maladies—"[17]

---

17 It is entirely possible that Hameiri uses the surname de Barbanel to denote Don Isaac Abarbanel (1437-1508), Portuguese statesman, philosopher, Bible commentator, and

The baroness's entire body shakes. She tenses her muscles, uproots her legs, clears her throat as if it was blocked by some rag or other, and bursts into a powerful, terrible yell.

"Doctor!! Doctor! They are laughing at me! These accursed ones are abusing me!! My rebellious daughter!! Doctor!!"

She snatches the revolver and begins to fire, to fire, to fire at her daughter, at Piotr Ilyich, at Fräulein Shabata, one after the other.

She faints and falls to the ground.

The next morning, when old Piotr Ilyich and Fräulein de Barbanel arrive at the cemetery, they find three corpses wallowing in blood.

Dr. Domshivski

The officer.

Baroness Medusa von Schinken.

The baroness lies with breasts exposed, a blue scar in the middle of her forehead. A puddle of congealed blood runs from her face and neck to her dead heart.

Odessa, 5680 (1919/1920).

---

financier. It is said that Abarbanel offered Ferdinand and Isabella six hundred thousand crowns for the revocation of the 1492 Jewish expulsion edict. Ferdinand hesitated, but was prevented from accepting the offer by Torquemada, the grand inquisitor, who rushed into the royal presence and, throwing a crucifix down before the king and queen, asked whether, like Judas, they would betray their Lord for thirty pieces of silver. In the end, Abarbanel managed only to get the date for the expulsion to be extended by two days.

On Fascism and Its Goal[1]

(Speech at the ceremonial opening of the Second National "Antifa" Conference in Tel Aviv, April 12, 1935 at Mugrabi Theater)

I would like you to feel a sixtieth part of how I feel each time I think of the Fascist movement and the goal whose banner it raises so proudly: *war*.

I would like to be able to instill into you the human terror that accompanies me like a terrible ghoul, that defiles my very existence every day I live on this earth. So that you can feel and know the precise nature of the concept that you use in your arguments and theoretical discussions and which you oppose, without knowing its true essence. Because how could you, young people, who started to live after the war, and those who have not participated in it because of age, know what war is?

For this reason, you cannot even imagine the war that has passed, or the one that is to come—that war about whose plans you continuously read about in the newspapers. For example, you think that all the abominations of war lie simply in death—at the time when a bullet pierces the brain or the heart, and the man drops down and dies. No, friends, that is not all! No artist in the world has the power to describe even a thousandth of what is known to you as the fear of death. But before this abomination, for which each man waits every minute—while still full of life, eternal strength, love, and plans for the future—there is a preceding abomination—the rule of man! The rule of officers, who compel their servants and those of lower rank to drink from their spittoon, vomit, and then drink again. What do you know of the nature of man's inhumanity to man? Of the wild enjoyment that the officer-monster in the form of a man relishes at the expense of his weaker victim at the front and during the general rule of war?! What do you know of His Majesty's officer, who puts to shame every beast in the world with his wild behavior, even

---

1   Avigdor Hameiri, "Al HaFashizm VeSio: HaMilhama" (Tel Aviv: Association for the Assistance of Victims of Fascism and Antisemitism "Antifa," May 1935), 3-8.

breaking nature's laws—the law of the jungle. The law of the jungle teaches us that when natural disasters such as thunder, lightning, and fire come to a city, animals know no hate, and all of them cling and hide together—the lion with the antelope, the leopard with the zebra—and don't hurt each other. But man—man—precisely at the hour of shared abomination, when a thousand deaths await you every second, when a thousand death-dealing bullets (called Satan's claws by soldiers) whistle past your ear, it is at this hour that the desire arises in the officer-monster to rule over you, abuse you, pick his brain for all sorts of tricks to torture you, and mock your powerlessness and terrible suffering. This horror in which you cannot tell which is worse—the pain or the shame. You feel only one thing with every fiber of your being—disgust, nauseating disgust so severe that it makes you want to vomit. This abomination, that kills every ounce of faith in the "homeland," the "homeland's misfortune," and the need to "defend the people of your nation" and your "homeland." Before a piece of shrapnel tears into your body, before you take the last breath of your young life, something else dies within you—patriotism, homeland, heroism, all the other things with whose beauty you always deceive yourself, and for which you think it at times even worthwhile to sacrifice your life for someone or something in a war like this! Lies! Lies! Lies! There is no heroism, no beauty, no enthusiasm, no desire to suffer and die. Look at your officers, your stomach will heave, and you will withdraw, to vomit and weep.

During one of my discussions with my friends, the creators of Jewish fascism in Israel, I asked their leader[2] if he has ever felt the double responsibility implicit in war: 1) responsibility to himself, to his own life, that is to say those whom he loves and whose love depends on him—his wife, sons, mother, brothers, and friends who fear for his life; 2) responsibility to others—the simple, upright men under his command who risk dying a gruesome death at any moment. I knew that he had never felt this in his life. I knew that he had never in his life stood face to face with awful death and never experienced the grisly death of others. It was enough for me to read his book about the Jewish Legion,[3] to sense that he had never been at the front in his life. It is difficult to deceive us on this point—we, who came so close to death, not once but

---

2   Vladimir (Ze'ev) Jabotinsky (1880-1940).

3   Ze'ev Jabotinsky, *Megil Hagedud,* trans. Abba Ahimeir (Jerusalem: Shutafut Hasolel, 1929); The Jewish Legion (1917–1921) was an unofficial name used to refer to five battalions of Jewish volunteers, the Thirty-Eighth to Forty-Second (Service) Battalions of

several times during the war. It is sufficient for us to hear a short sentence from someone about the war to recognize that, for him, it is only a theoretical concept. When I was at the front, we heard a rumor that the German poet Richard Dehmel had volunteered for the front.[4] I said: let's see. His first poem written on the front will tell us where he is located. And so it was. When the first poem arrived we knew at once that this fervent patriot was serving a good distance away from the front and from death. He had not yet had the opportunity of seeing any of his friends suddenly, in the midst of conversation, falling pale, dumb, with dimmed eyes, never to rise or smile again, never to answer when his dear name was called out . . .

My aim is to convince you of the above, to poison you with the villainy of that "beautiful" life and hectic abomination of war, so that you vomit out every kind of pretty slogan and every poem about war and about heroism, and about all the other things that prepare you to become holy cannon fodder again!

Fascism doesn't come like a thief at midday, attacking you suddenly with the coarseness of a drunken murderer. No, my friends! Fascism is a refined diplomat who sneaks into your soul, mind, and blood like an intoxicating fragrance, in a thousand different ways that you don't feel at all. Fascism has the special talent of using the best and most beautiful part of your young souls, playing delicate tunes on your heart strings, and weaving spiders' webs around your souls that slowly strangle you and silence your healthy logic with utter confidence. It even uses the "ideal," that holy of holies of the human soul, to tempt you. Sometimes it comes in the form of "love of the homeland," sometimes as "noble, lofty heroism," sometimes as "one hundred percent genuine Hebrew work," even as "faith as pure and holy as the glow of the heavens." Even I was tempted by it when I arrived in Israel! I said to myself: here conditions are different. Here we must build a Jewish state which should and must serve as an example for all other countries in the world. I started to give up my human ideals for a historical moment, because of the beautiful ideal of a Jewish state, and because of that ideal of ideals and dream of dreams: Hebrew culture. Only when a quarter of my life had passed did I gradually realize for whom

---

the Royal Fusiliers, raised by the British army to fight against the Ottoman Empire during World War I.

4   Richard Dehmel (1863-1920), German poet and writer. Although fifty-one at the time, Dehmel volunteered in 1914 and served until 1916, when he was wounded. Hameiri is not being fair.

and for what I had given up everything for which my sacred soul had wailed and wondered: it was for the new Hebrew fascism that copies all the impurities in Europe in all its details! Do you know what we achieved in this field before the world war? Do you know that even before the war we understood, even under Austro-Hungarian rule, that an intelligent man would not sit at the same table as an officer in a coffee house?! Yes! You don't know that! When I wrote about it in *The Great Madness*[5] people laughed and it was called a literary joke! I wrote: "Who sits beside an officer? A whore or, worse, another officer."[6] You don't know that this was one of our best accomplishments before the war. Which man of intelligence would speak disrespectfully of Marxism before the war? It is difficult to imagine now, but it is a well-known fact, that everyone treated the general human ideal of socialism and its doctrine with respect. The Capitalists didn't refer to it at all because Capitalists don't use argument—their only theory is force. The philosopher, who at most rejected the scientific methodology of Marxism (not the idea itself), stood before the sanctity of the general socialist idea with dignity, like other scientific endeavors such as Darwinism, Mendelism, or Freudianism.[7] It was possible to oppose it, but no man of logic or ethics could speak about it with disrespect.

And today—today after the war? Every impure leper spits on the ideal of Marxism, on its very ideal! This is where they start! Without any knowledge of the socialist doctrine, tactually sitting down for an hour and studying the ABCs of Marxism, they declare openly, without shame or fear of appearing ridiculous: I don't want to know anything about socialism! Do you realize the stupidity of this reply? They complain about Hitler that he knows nothing about Judaism—but they themselves dishonor something that is far from their intellectual and ethical comprehension. They complain that Hitler burns books—but they themselves, if you give them the same power for a single day, they would consign the whole of Jewish culture to the flames together with the language itself and everyone who opposes their sick ethics, including Isaiah,

---

5   Avigdor Hameiri, *Hashigaon Hagadol. Reshimot Katzin Ivri Bemilhama Hagedola* (Tel Aviv: Mitzpeh, 1929); Avigdor Hameiri, *The Great Madness*, ed. Peter C. Appelbaum and trans. Jacob Freedman and Yael Lotan (Middletown, RI: Stone Tower Press and Boston, MA: Black Widow Press, 2021).

6   Hameiri, *The Great Madness*, 116.

7   Charles Darwin (1809-1882), naturalist, geologist, and biologist, best known for his contributions to the science of evolution; Gregor Mendel (1882-1884), founder of the modern science of genetics; Sigmund Freud (1856-1939), founder of modern psychoanalysis.

Amos, and Elijah the Prophet! Because it's a little difficult to fake or emasculate Isaiah and the Prophets and turn them into sword-polishing officer lickspittles! No, not them!

Now the heroes of Jewish fascism will, I know, burst out of their lairs with their herd of dogs, and point their fingers at me: look, he is making common cause with those who hate Hebrew culture! As if they have any connection with the culture—if there is something called Hebrew culture at all. I do not speak here in the name of any party. I have carefully preserved my socialist ideal even at a time when I was forced to work for non-socialist newspapers, who, by the way, never thought of equating Marxism with infamy. My socialist ideal always seeks its counterpart in every party and movement, in the same way it sought it in revisionism until it became too right wing. I speak here in the name of the deep inner revulsion that damages my entire life, I speak about the human impurity called war, about which Fascists shamelessly boast, and which our Hebrew Fascists imitate with buttons[8] and straps, confusing our youth who haven't tasted war even in their dreams. I don't participate actively in the work of any party. But when I die and the Fascists and warmongers come knocking on my grave, I will spit my bitter, aching disgust on those who rob me of rest even in my grave. I will rise up from my grave to warn you against this loathsome poison that your children soak up without proper knowledge of what is happening by their parents and teachers, who have not yet trodden the path on which fascism steals into young, impressionable brains. It is also a matter of beautiful literature and its doctrine—a literature that doesn't know in the service of whom or what it stands. It has a special name: l'art pour l'art, art for the sake of art. L'art pour l'art! They write beautiful poems in praise of life and nature, covering over the ugliness of suffering and subjugation! L'art pour l'art! They write poems about human bravery and the loyalty of the mother who has buried ten beautiful healthy sons, sacrificed to the homeland, and who received a gift from His Majesty, covering up the poor woman's face twisted with grief and wet with tears, after she has been left barren and without any reason for living or dying! L'art pour l'art! They write love poems about a youth and his beloved that make sure to emphasize the young woman's pride in the beloved of her heart, who died a martyr's death on the homeland's altar. They cover disgust at the slaughter, and the tragedy of a young woman who commits

---

8   "His Majesty's Buttons" is Hameiri's sarcastic reference to officers (see Hameiri, *The Great Madness*, 116-122).

suicide at the grave of her beloved—if she even knows where it is! And finally, L'art pour l'art! They write poetry about heroes and bravery, wishing thereby to cover up the wretched wormlike human being who is cast half-alive into a lime pit while still breathing, and left there to rot, while his wife and sons can't even fall weeping onto his grave because they don't know where it is! These poets practice their refined art in the coffee houses of the city, accompanied by the aroma of a strong cup of espresso or a glass of good red wine.

They stuff your children with such art so that they grow up and go like lambs to the slaughter in the factories of shared arms manufacturers in all the countries! I don't want you to think that I advise against sending your children to school, because there is no other alternative to teach your children Hebrew as well as general culture. But I wish that you could inoculate your children with an antidote against the plague called "culture of the homeland," whose sole purpose is to sacrifice them like sheep on the altar of the unappeasable appetite of the Capitalist Moloch![9] I wish that a mother could, together with sweet mother's milk, feed her children on the cyanide of imprisoned hate for the stupidity of war and fascism in general. Hate for the entire culture of war that dares to speak of heroism and the national culture, that sanctifies war and raises its desolate abomination to God!

Oh, if only the teachers knew as well what war is! And those who knew, if only they had not forgotten, in their temporary doze, what they had felt at the front and near it and around it! For then they would have put at the top of their educational doctrine the ancient-modern doctrine: the doctrine of bitter hate and deep disdain for all the world's ideals that agree for even a split second to war.

This is not the place to suggest theories, or preach a socialist sermon. I have come in an attempt to save your young and tender lives from going to a living grave, to prevent you from breaking your beautiful lives in the middle and agreeing to rot in a lime pit in the midst of work and the ascent of your tender lives! Each one of you has a duty to himself to fight with all means possible against the Fascist plague that incites everyone to war. Each one in his own way, by his own means and talents, but especially by opening the eyes of the youth with knowledge, by educating them on socialist science which enlightens you in all the secrets of life and creation! If only such progressive humaneness had arisen generations ago, to fight a holy war against this

---

9   Canaanite god who was the recipient of child sacrifice.

contagion—which constantly changes its form and speaks in terms of high and lofty human ideals—perhaps we wouldn't now be confronted with the abomination that approaches us anew with all its horrors. Then our youth would have known that if there was to be a war, if there was to be heroism and victory, let it be a comprehensible war, with logic, form, and noble heroism. That would be a war for my own life and good, for my own homeland and my ideals! War for a free life of work, and creativity without the rule of money, without the rule of government ministers, counts and dukes, who send you off to war while they themselves live the good life, wasting all the treasures of humanity, and your own handiwork, in pursuit of their sick harlotry! If there is a war, let it be for the general human ideal, for the only ideal that has the logical and philosophical underpinnings worthy of the name "ideal." Because the meaning of the word *ideal* is an effort to achieve three attributes: *something good that doesn't yet exist, something that is good for society, and something that is good for me as well.* The ideal of an advanced man is *to live a happy life in a happy society*, not to live happy as a pig in clover, in a starving society, suffering and lacking even the most minimal human rights! By all means go—and die, if necessary, for the first ideal! But not for any other war, not for a war which champions the rule of pig-like men over other men, which promotes the abuse of millions! For man has one characteristic that raises him up above all other creatures—*shame*, in other words *contrition*. To live during our time of advanced civilization together with the disgrace of all disgraces—*war*—can only be described by the word *shame*! Try to delve deep into your feelings when you see an airplane flying high in the sky on a clear day or a dark night. Look at this glorious spectacle and search your souls to see whether this lofty feeling isn't interrupted by an ache mixed with deep shame: this glorious human achievement that brings a little beauty, happiness, and usefulness to wretched humanity has been created only for death! To hurl bombs on our heads and blow up young children playing happily in the street.

Shame! Shame! Shame! Oy vavoy to our lives!

We must scream with all our strength, and whisper burning words in each other's ears, against a war for such "culture" and "ideals": Don't go! Don't go! Don't go! Better to die on the spot than go and die over there or even to return like a leprous dog, living for generations for the next war like a leprous dog and then dying like a leprous dog!

Learn the bitterest, most obstinate slogan of all: *Don't go! Don't go! Don't go!*

About the Translators

Peter Appelbaum is a retired microbiologist who is spending his retirement years writing and translating books about Jewish history during World War I and the immediate post-war period. He is the recipient of the 2019 Rise Domb Porjes prize for his translation of Avigdor Hameiri's *Hell on Earth*.

Dan Hecht is a doctoral student at the School of Cultural Studies at Tel Aviv University who wrote an extensive Masters thesis on the writings of Avigdor Hameiri, focusing on his dual national loyalty to his Hungarian heritage and his Hebrew homeland. He is currently writing his PhD on the essayistic prose of Eliezer Steinmann.